ACTS OF GRACE

MASCOT
BOOKS

www.mascotbooks.com

ACTS OF GRACE

For more information, please contact:
Mascot Books, an imprint of Amplify Publishing Group
620 Herndon Parkway, Suite 320
Herndon, VA 20170
info@mascotbooks.com

Library of Congress Control Number: 2021921769

CPSIA Code: PRV0722A
ISBN-13: 978-1-63755-290-2

Printed in the United States

For Emily
November 26, 1995 – November 6, 2021

And for those who fight invisible battles.

You're not alone.

This book is for you.

ACTS OF GRACE

A NOVEL

SYDNEY WALTERS

PROLOGUE

EVERY NOW AND THEN, a hapless herd of deer wander into the town. Tired and hungry, they begin their journey just south of the Susquehanna River, passing through the forest-rich game lands, and silently trekking through the surrounding farmland toward the uninviting gray woodland that Centralia has to offer them.

The journey is just another obstacle to overcome in their life-long search of food and a safe place to make their bed. Stealthily, the herds move in unison day and night through the green game lands, consuming as much of it as they can without being spotted by a larger, stronger animal, until they place a hoof onto the dark, weakened earth of Centralia, below which a much larger, stronger force lurks.

There's nothing for the deer there. The trees are bare, lifeless corpses frozen in time against a smoky blur. There is no brush left for them to graze upon, but some of them still choose to press through to the other side, where the grass is always greener. Some of them will make it. Some of them won't.

It's a gamble they have to take, by nature, of course. They move forward by instinct. If word could be passed around the herds to avoid the area or turn back to the more forgiving game lands, then perhaps even the deer would be laughing at Centralia's ever-stubborn town folk. They would click and grunt to each other, *"Who the hell would go there?"*

I wonder sometimes if the deer were to travel south from the hunting paths only to find themselves at the outskirts of a burning town, would they risk crossing the river with the threat of a fiery death? Or would they turn back and risk being left at the mercy of a hunter?

My daydreams and nightmares about Centralia were becoming more and more lucid.

CHAPTER ONE

I HAD DISCOVERED THAT working under Mr. Duncan could be frivolous. I met him at the office every morning at nine o'clock sharp. He waited for me at his desk with only one library lamp illuminating his face and glasses, which was my signal to turn on all the lights.

"Good morning, Mr. Duncan."

"Good morning, Grace, and . . . again, calling me Nick is *fine*."

Nick was unashamedly and undoubtedly the world's greatest professor-turned-editor, a job he hadn't had for too long, but apparently long enough to hire an assistant.

Assist him, I did, but it was not quite the work I had expected. After I turned on the lights, I headed to the coffee machine in the corner. I flipped the switch, and a red-orange light greeted me with its routine click. As the water heated up, I prepared the ex-professor's mug for him. It was sleek, tall, and black; the opposite of how he liked his coffee.

I grabbed two sugar packets from a ramekin and sprinkled them into the mug first. Then, I emptied two single-serving creamer containers on top of the sugar. The coffee came last, but not to be poured all the way to the rim. Three quarters of the way was just fine, he said. Lastly, I mixed the contents with a stir stick and left it in the cup for him, in case his hands got fidgety later. It was an odd combination of actions, but it wasn't hard to get down. I did this three times every day: in the morning, before lunch, and once more to power through the last hour of work.

I also made a cup for myself three times a day. My mug was much smaller than his—a white porcelain mug with a dove on it. I poured the coffee first and added just one sugar, no cream. Then I stirred it up and threw away the stick.

We were Stark Publishing Company. When not coffee-making, the rest of my day consisted of reading through queries sent by mail and passing them along to our publisher, Mr. Henry Winger. Wearing what looks like the same black suit and tie every day, Henry was a very tall, very broad Philadelphian with dark hair, dark eyes, and an aura of seniority. If the manuscripts were to his liking, they eventually got passed along to Mr. Duncan—*Nick*—for editing. Stark Publishing, being located in such a big city, received publishing queries daily, and I got to read through each and every one of them. This is the part I enjoyed the most. Budding writers sent in their books, be it a fantasy novel or a cookbook, and I read through them all, sometimes twice over if the story was particularly riveting. The gates to their bookish dreams were opened by me, and then the books reached Nick, who cracked his knuckles and began to scan the work for edits. Unfortunately, I didn't get to do much of that. I read, I passed along, and I waited. But I, too, had the passion in my heart to write and write again.

Tap. Tap. Tap.

Sometimes I couldn't help it. The pen I got as a graduation present was often used more as a musical instrument than a writing instrument. I tapped it against papers, against the side of my leg, my mug, my lips, but most of all, my little desk.

At the corner of the office, I sat in the shadow of a large mahogany executive desk with a dominating black leather chair. My desk was a light brown secretary-style desk, attached to the wall with an assortment of cubbies, one drawer, and a white rolling chair pulled underneath. While my desk piled with envelopes, Nick's piled with manuscripts, overflowing from his inbox and outbox and all but hiding his glossy black typewriter, an old but durable piece of his soul, comparable to Ernest Hemingway's Royal Quiet Deluxe typewriter.

The environment supported the hierarchy, with me at the bottom, but I couldn't complain, or I simply chose not to. Sooner or later, Nick would speak up.

"Grace."

"Hm?"

"It's a little distracting, the tapping."

"Oh, right. Sorry."

At that point, I would have my second cup of coffee a little earlier in the day.

CHAPTER TWO

IF IT WAS NOT ALREADY ON HIS DESK, I brought the newspaper to Nick in the morning. Maybe it was a little cliché, but we liked to discuss current events with our first coffee of the day. While it may have been just small talk to him, I found it intriguing. I was still getting used to a daily paper with different news every day, never the same stories as the day before.

"Anything piquing your interest today, Grace?" Nick asked when I brought him the paper one particular day.

I skimmed the headlines for the most surprising story. *Jackpot.*

"July 1980. A teenager was found guilty of murdering his fellow student."

"Oh, *Christ*," Nick said rubbing his forehead.

I continued to read.

"There was a love affair. The guy's gal wasn't being true, and he was hurt badly by it, so he *shot* the boy she was with, three times in the stomach."

"Oh, *Jesus* Christ," he repeated.

"It sounds like a bad romance novel," I remarked.

"Ah, yes. Anything you might like to write more on?"

I gave my weakest, most pathetic laugh. "Yeah, maybe."

I could feel Nick staring at me while I fidgeted with my pen. He leaned back in his seat.

"You know, Grace. You've been here three weeks now."

I nodded.

"Have you been writing anything?"

"I have."

But it wasn't the entire truth. I had written down a few of my thoughts, a few reminders, grocery lists, along with a letter that I *wanted* to send home to my family . . . but no writing of substance.

Nick continued to peer at me. "Is there anything you'd like to show me?"

"Not yet," I admitted.

Nick looked disappointed, but also curious. I know he expects more of me, to come up with my own query, I suppose. I'm in the right place for it, after all. I guess I just haven't been very inspired lately, just pouring all this coffee and reading other writers' works. It's easy getting lost in a book, but writing on your own is hard.

Nick neatly folded up his paper and swapped it for a thick manuscript from his pile of works, adjusting his glasses accordingly. So, I turned back to my desk to sip my coffee in my solitude. I had three unopened queries to my left, but in an attempt to find something more interesting to talk about at lunch, I fixed my eyes on the newspaper.

Articles about public appearances made by President Jimmy Carter and news of construction work flourishing throughout Philadelphia reigned over the front page. It was nothing that truly interested or excited me, and I didn't know enough to touch on either topic. *Oh, well,* I thought. *Perhaps tomorrow will bring another event, crisis, or breaking story to linger on.*

CHAPTER THREE

Upon returning home, I was greeted at the door by my boyfriend, Joseph. He finished work about an hour before me at his father's firm, so it was always a nice way to end the day.

"Hey there."

"Hey, Joe, what do ya know?"

He pulled me in for a quick peck before shutting the door behind us.

"Hello!" I shouted across the foyer to Emilia and Richard, but they were busy discussing whatever it is they discuss in the evening sitting upon their lounge chairs, Richard holding a whiskey, and Emilia a glass of chardonnay.

"How was your day?" asked Joseph.

"It was . . . good. We got three queries today."

"Oh, anything piquing your interest?"

I paused at his words before saying, "You know, Mr. Duncan asked me the exact *same* thing today."

"You really should call him Nick now, Grace," he added playfully.

I sighed, "I know, I know. It's . . . it's . . ."

"What is it?"

"It's just . . . I don't feel like we're—like we're . . ."

"Equals?" Joseph asked in that mindreading love language of his. I smiled at the words.

"How do you do that? You always know—"

"Just what to say?"

I gave him a playful pinch on his arm, and he returned a laugh.

"But, really, Grace. You *just* started working there. It's going to take some time, but what will really count is your attitude toward it all."

Joseph was right, and I knew it all along, but I guess I still felt like an outsider sometimes.

"I just wonder when it will *feel* like I'm a part of it, *truly* a part of the company."

"Whenever you make it that way, Grace."

We stared into each other's eyes, and then I removed my bag to hang it on the hook by the door and let my hair down. Together we made our way upstairs to the bedroom, and I gravitated toward the writing desk. Joseph sat on the edge of the bed.

"Oh, do you want me to give you some space?" he asked me sweetly.

"What? No, no, Joseph, it's your house. You don't have to—"

"*Ours*," he interrupted.

A reminder that I still need every now and then.

"I'm going to start making some dinner," he said, casually. He is far too polite.

I closed my eyes and smiled. "Ok, *dear*," I mocked. He flashed me a smile and then headed down the stairs to the kitchen.

I had been writing a letter to my mother and stepfather Bill, even though I knew it could never be sent, with their zip code being removed off the face of the earth. But it still felt good to type. Since having them spend the day here with all of us, I missed them terribly. I'd spent four years away from them at university, but knowing they had retreated to that awful town left me grasping at the air trying to pull them back. They promised they'd return, and they promised they'd consider moving.

In the letter, I explained that Pennsylvania was bustling with coal miners, something I had learned in the paper. So, I knew that there would be other work for Bill to take on . . . but it wasn't him I had to convince. My mother, still set in her ways, won a personal victory in visiting the city. It was triumphant, and everyone agreed. But it wasn't enough for me. Sure, she'd visit again—I was confident enough in that.

I'd circled various apartments in newspapers, ones that were affordable in the city. I'd researched mines just outside of Philadelphia, in Centerport, or Fullerton, or Bridgeton, so that Bill could easily find work. I found an auto body shop that could repair even Bill's old beater of a car. I even found a new boutique down the street from my office that was full of beautiful summer dresses my mom would love to wear.

I laid it all out in a letter that I could never send. While letter writing may be therapeutic, I knew I should be writing something worth reading, something with legs. It was a pain in my ass, this writer's block. Especially because I had a degree to lean on now, and I wanted to . . . no, *needed* to put it to good use. So, I just stared out the window, as one does.

"Grace?"

I snapped out of my reverie when Joseph appeared at the door.

"Mhmm?"

"Phone call."

I jumped up, kissing Joseph on the cheek as I barreled past him on my way down the steps to the kitchen. I only got phone calls from one person.

"Hello?"

"*Grace!* How are ya, kiddo?"

"Hi, Dad," I said holding back my joy on hearing Bill's voice. "How are things?"

"Oh, you know, the usual. Your mother is around the corner, resting in bed. But, uh, she says hello."

"Oh . . . well, will you tell her I said hi?"

"Will do, kiddo. Listen, uh, I wanted to tell you about something I saw the other day."

"Oh, what is it?"

Dad paused for just a moment.

"There was this *deer.*"

I twisted the phone cord in my hand as I looked over to Joseph's parents in the living room, sitting oh-so contented.

"It was all alone, just wandering through the yard this afternoon. I couldn't believe my eyes."

"A *deer*?"

"Yeah, a deer! It was a buck, too! So, I went outside to get a closer look."

"What happened?"

"Well, when I took a step into the yard, there was a *whole group* of them! Just behind the buck, maybe, oh, I don't know, five or six of them. They were all following the buck. You really had to be there, Grace."

"That's incredible, Dad! I, uh, wish I could have been there to see it," I lied.

"Yeah, they seem to be hanging around the area. It seems like, like they might feel safe here," he continued.

Safe? In Centralia?

Herds rarely ever passed through it. I thought of my daydream, and then felt my heart drop to my stomach. I didn't know what to say, and I feared I had created an uncomfortable silence.

"Well, anyway, kiddo. Just a little update is all. I love you, Grace. Hope you're enjoying your new job."

"Thanks, Dad. I am . . . and I love you, too."

This call left me feeling a little raw, and my stomach went sour. I thought maybe I should just get some rest. So, I headed back up the stairs.

Joseph passed me as he headed back into the kitchen. "Hungry?

"Uh, not right now. You go ahead."

"Are you sure?"

"Mhmm."

It was about the only thing I was sure of at that moment.

CHAPTER FOUR

I SWITCHED ON ALL THE LIGHTS, then I made Nick his coffee and one for myself. I brought in the paper, set it on his desk, and began twirling my pen.

"I was thinking," Nick began, "that you might be interested in one of my novels."

"Oh, well, yes, I think I would," I said.

Nick shot me a knowing look. "I used to be like you, you know, unsure of myself in a brand new world. So, I bought this here typewriter and wrote about the world that *I* wanted to live in."

He removed his glasses and let them hang around his neck on a string, running a hand over the typewriter. "My fantasies came to be on a blank page, with my fingertips being the touch of God that brought them to life. Mysteries, crime, suspense."

I was surprised at this piece of information. I had always taken him for a *War and Peace* type of author; a classics guy.

"I'd love to read your work."

"Or maybe not," he added.

Confused, I raised an eyebrow in protest.

"Maybe it's not a good time, since you're busy with *your* writing," he said.

I felt that lump in my throat again and swallowed past it, but ended up inhaling some of my coffee and started coughing. As a diversion from his comments and implied criticism, I pointed to a random news piece I had found with an odd title: *The Rise of the Georgia Guidestones*. Still coughing, I asked, "Did you hear about this?" I pointed to the title.

Nick shook his head and attached his glasses back onto his face. He was playing along with my charade a little *too* well. "Never heard of it. Why, do *you* know something about it, Grace?"

I bent lower into the paper, clearing my coffee-filled airway and began to read the article out loud: "*A large monument has been created and presented in Elbert County, Georgia. Multiple slabs of granite with a capstone slab stand engraved with a set of guidelines on how to recreate society in a post-apocalyptic world . . .*"

My words trailed off into a mumble, but my mind was in the grip of the print. The piece described a set of ten short rules on how to rebuild and maintain a population after a horrible event, or the apocalypse. One of the rules stuck out to me the most:

Protect people and nations with fair laws and just courts.

"Grace?" Nick asked.

I wasn't daydreaming this time. I was lost in the story. "Sorry, I just . . . It's interesting, is all."

"Maybe we should get back to work," he suggested.

I nodded and turned back to my desk, looking over to the unopened queries. I folded the newspaper, but I hadn't finished reading the article yet. Something about it just seemed so . . . so relevant to me. With a turn of my head and a not-so-discreet flip of my hair, I saw that Nick was buried in a manuscript behind me, so I quickly tucked the newspaper away in my bag to take home later.

When I got home that evening, I planned to head straight up to the bedroom. Richard and Emilia were having some friends over for a get together, and Joseph was down the stairs mingling with all of them. I managed to slip past them unnoticed and was tiptoeing past the kitchen when the phone rang. Everyone was chatting away in the living room, and nobody could hear it ring, so I made my way over and picked it up.

"Hello?"

"Grace? Is that *you*?"

"Dad?"

"Oh, thank *goodness*. Grace, I—I just. I needed to . . ."

"What's wrong? Dad, are you alright?"

"I—I haven't told your mother."

"Told her what, Dad?"

"I couldn't tell her. The *deer*."

"What about the deer?"

"The buck, Grace. I saw it on my way to the tunnels. It was . . . it was—"

"Dad?"

"It was sticking out of the ground. There was smoke all around it, it must've gotten stuck."

He paused for a moment.

"It was dead, Grace. It was *burned alive*."

The room faded to black around me. Dad sounded like he was about to burst into tears, but instead he talked through it, mumbling and breathing hard.

"I thought he'd be ok leading the herd, but I was wrong. I didn't think it would happen to me again. I didn't think I would *see* it."

"Dad, I—"

"I always knew you were right, Grace, about this place. I know I never said it, but I always *knew*. But your mother, no matter what happens . . . she *won't* go, Grace. I, I just don't know what I can do anymore."

Even after Sam died, Bill held it all together. He always held it together, and he did it for my mother. I'd never heard him so distraught.

"Dad, just *breathe*. I—I . . ." I searched for the words. "I'm sorry.

I'm so, so sorry that you had to see it. I know how it . . . *looks*."

He exhaled heavily into the phone.

"You know that I want to fix this, Dad. I wish I could make it all go away."

"Oh, Grace," he pleaded, "I wish you could, too."

After the call, my brain was cycling through the same three scenes: the buck leading the herd through the woods; then, the buck falling through the ground, half burnt and crying out; then, Sam slipping away through my fingers, falling down into the gaping road.

I couldn't control my breathing. That lump in my throat was growing larger and larger until I could barely suck in the air. I paced across the kitchen through the foyer, quickly without being seen by Joseph and tripped up the stairs. When I got to the bedroom, I shut the door behind me. Out of sight and out of earshot, I kicked the door *hard*. It didn't leave a mark, and I was grateful for that.

I was infuriated at it all. It seemed to never end, the suffering. There was always more pain to feel as long as there were feet on top of Centralia, whether it be my family's pain or a herd of deer's.

I strode over to my writing desk and pulled the newspaper out of my bag with sweaty palms and traced a trembling finger across the page searching for the article.

Tap. Tap. Tap.

"*There*," I whispered.

I took a deep, necessary breath and skimmed to the place I had left off earlier. My vision switched from red, to black and white.

I read that the ten guidelines were engraved in eight different languages across each stone, so that lots of different folk would be able to read and understand them. They were meant to be interpreted as a sort of modernized Bible to rational thinking after a world-altering event. Below the listed guidelines was a quote that read: *"Let these be guidestones for an age of reason."*

The words resonated with me, and I felt a twinkle in my eye.

Centralia is what I would consider post-apocalyptic, and if it *were* to be rebuilt, like my dear Sam would have wanted, it would be a just and fair town full of people who want the best for their fellow townsfolk, not just themselves.

But I didn't think that it was a place that would stand a chance of any recovery for the years, decades, or even centuries to come. Not as long as the fire kept burning below. My family deserved better than what they had, and those who were killed in the fire, whether it was from the initial blast or from the ground collapsing underneath them, deserved to have their voices heard. Then maybe one day, when the fire died out, the town could be reclaimed and rebuilt using these guidelines, with liberty and justice for all.

That's it, I said to myself. *This is what I've been waiting for. I know what I want to write about now, and why should I hide it any longer? I'm no mystery writer or cookbook author. My writing doesn't have to be in a fantasy genre in order to describe the world that I want to live in, and it doesn't have to be some sob story of an essay, like the personal narrative I wrote in my freshman year. I can write it exactly for what it is: the hard truth.*

I placed a fresh sheet of paper into the carriage of my typewriter, wiped the sweat from my hands, cracked my knuckles, and began.

CHAPTER FIVE

I PASSED OUT AT MY DESK. Joseph had been calling me to come down for dinner until he decided to just come upstairs and grab me. I woke up to his hand on the nape of my neck, and it scared the hell out of me.

"It's just me!" he said.

I sighed and rubbed my forehead.

"I was calling for you. I didn't even see you come in. Is everything alright?"

My eyes adjusted to the papers in front of me. I collected them all in my hands. In just over an hour, I had written eight pages on the horrors of life in Centralia, from the mining accident to the dead buck. It all just poured out of me like my morning coffee.

"What's all this?" he asked.

I quickly turned toward him, stiff as a board, and my neck cracked in opposition.

"Joe, I think I've *done* it. I have a story."

"Wait, what do you mean? You . . . you're going to publish this? What is it about?"

"What do you *think*?" I asked.

He was staring at my papers, all crumpled and smeared with ink that hadn't dried, and then to my hands, which were shaking.

"How about we grab a bite to eat? Or, do you want to just go to bed?" he suggested.

Confused at his response, I looked down at my work. It was *such* a mess. I could spot the errors a mile away. My hands shook, and I noticed that I had been picking away at my old scar. I felt embarrassed at the unsightly vision I'd become, so I shoved the papers into my bag that had, at some point fallen, onto the floor.

"Right, that's probably a good idea."

He offered me his hand, steady and warm, and walked me to the bed. Then he picked up my bag to hang on the hook by the front door.

"Wait," I pleaded. "Could you leave it here?"

He didn't protest, and instead walked over to the desk and placed it by my typewriter. He looked concerned, to say the least. "Grace, are you ok?"

Aside from the phone call from Bill, the stiff neck, and the aching fingers? I thought. "Yeah, I'm ok."

Convinced for the time being, Joseph took off his glasses and joined me in bed. Within a minute, I was asleep.

———

The next day, I got into work a little earlier, around eight-thirty. I wanted to catch Nick before we were punched in on the clock. This would clash with Joseph's work schedule, and I didn't want to bother him for anything, so instead of being dropped off, I decided to take the bus.

Just as I arrived, I caught Nick at the door. He said, "Grace? You're *early*."

"I have some news," I replied.

"Well, I hope it's the newspaper. Did you happen to take yesterday's paper *home*?"

I ignored the question. We both rushed to get inside, me with my collection of papers clutched to my chest and him with an obvious question mark on his face.

"What's going on?" he asked.

"I've written something. Something big, I think."

"Well!" he exclaimed. "Let's have a look at it then."

I smiled at his enthusiasm. "Ok, yes, but first let me say that I wrote it all at once, and it's a little messy and—"

"Good thing I'm an editor, then."

I stacked the papers against his desk and promptly handed them to him. He adjusted his glasses, and I gravitated toward the coffee machine.

After some time, and two fresh cups of coffee later, he set down my work. I had been watching him pass over each page, which he did with almost no expression at all, and it only added to the suspense. Time was ticking, and I just needed to know what he was thinking.

"Grace . . ."

"Yes?"

"You seem to have written an exposé."

I inhaled. "Yes, I believe so."

He licked his forefinger and flipped through the pages, skimming them. I sat at my desk and waited, feeling like all my insides had spilled out on the floor in front of him. A silence fell over the room.

"It needs some work, but it is engrossing."

I exhaled. "So, it *piques your interest* then?" I asked mischievously. He smirked. "It does indeed."

He took a sip from his mug and leaned back in his chair, staring off into the distance. I also took a sip from my coffee and waited. He was contemplating something.

"I'm going to do you a favor, Miss Grace."

I straightened up in my seat and set my mug down.

"I can edit this to the best of my ability, but once I've finished, I want you to present it to Henry."

I looked over to Henry's door. "To Mr. Winger? But it's not a novel query . . ."

"Henry has some connections with *The Philadelphian*, and I believe that might be the best option for you with this piece."

"Yes, I agree."

The Philadelphian is the city's most read paper, and it is a prestigious one. To publish an article about Centralia in *The Philadelphian*, or any newspaper, was something I had been longing for since I was a child. Not *one* major news outlet wrote anything about the blast, and it was about damn time that people knew what *really* happened to Centralia and what goes on today in that town.

Nick placed my papers at the top of his inbox, then took a few swigs from his mug and studied me, eyes squinting under two glass frames. "You wrote all this last night, you say?"

"I did," I admitted.

Nick huffed out all the air in his lungs, and then produced a wicked, maniacal laugh. He was genuinely laughing *at* me.

"What? What's so funny?" I asked defiantly.

"You, Miss Grace. *You* are!" He continued to laugh and shake his head. "I think you might be my favorite student. You've got guts, Grace."

I appreciated that with every ounce of my heart, and it showed. I couldn't help but blush. Nick did a quick spin in his large leather chair. "I'll start my edits today, but it will have to be after hours. In the meantime, you should think about what you'll want to say to Mr. Winger."

"Thank you, sir," I said earnestly.

"I *knew* you had it in you. We all have a story, Grace."

I smiled at him and felt the hair rise up on the back of my neck.

"Now, today is going to be a long day," he declared as he tossed back the remainder of his coffee and held out his mug to me. "I'm going to need another cup."

CHAPTER SIX

I HADN'T EATEN BREAKFAST OR LUNCH. So, upon returning home, feeling somewhat accomplished and ravenous, I offered to cook dinner for everyone.

Richard and Emilia, lovely and welcoming as they are, always kept the kitchen stocked with fresh fruit, veg, and a selection of cured meats, as well as milk, eggs, breads, jams, and (my personal favorite) delicious cherry pie.

I never really learned to cook more than maybe three dishes growing up, but making an effort was the least I could do for my second family in their astoundingly beautiful home. Luckily, a recent query I'd read for a cookbook included a recipe that had been engulfing my mind all day long. Emilia, Richard, and Joseph watched me wander around the kitchen with an assortment of expressions on their faces; confusion, shock, and admiration.

Finally, I rolled up my sleeves and began pounding away at pre-cut pieces of chicken breast, chopping up mushrooms, and searching for . . . what was it called, *Marchala* wine?

On the wall beside the kitchen phone was a shelf of wines displayed in order of what I assumed to be age and importance, ranging from bold and savory reds, to sweet and subtle whites, ending with the cooking wines, where my eyes met the endearing wine I'd been daydreaming about.

"Ah, *Marsala*," I noted.

After creating a mess of flour, mushroom bits, and sauce splatters, I wiped the sweat away from my brow, unknowingly smearing a glob of sauce on my forehead. I had a pot of rice ready to my left. Dinner was served!

"Ok, ok, I think it's ready!" I hollered.

Joseph stepped into the kitchen first after waiting very patiently for me to complete my first attempt at a home-cooked meal in my new home. He looked around the kitchen, eyes widening at the mess I had made, then looked into the pan, eyebrows lifting as he stared at the contents. Then he looked at my face and burst out laughing.

"What?"

"Your *face*, Grace."

I picked up the Marsala bottle and stared at my reflection in its glossy glass. "Right," I said, defeated and embarrassed at seeing the sauce on my forehead.

"I'll start cleaning up, and you three start eating," Joseph said.

We complied with our orders, grabbed a plate, glass, and serving spoon each, and finally landed at the table together.

"So, Miss Grace, what is the occasion?" Richard inquired.

I double checked my forehead with my hand for any remaining sauce before saying, "Well, I've written a piece on my hometown, and I'm hoping to have it published in *The Philadelphian*."

Emilia began tapping a fork to the side of her water glass as praise, and Richard motioned for her to stop. He said, "Excellent. Good work, Grace. I was beginning to think you'd lost your mind in that kitchen." He raised a forkful of chicken, examined it, popped it into his mouth and chewed. "Mmm. Well done with the Marsala, as well."

Afterward, against my wishes, Emilia insisted I go upstairs while she claimed the kitchen for washing up the rest of the dishes.

This was another accomplishment for the day. I wondered what

I could do to receive Joseph's congratulations, too. It was early days for celebration, but I wanted to show my gratitude for Joseph, and his family most of all. Joseph and I lay in bed together, both stuffed to the gullet with our hands intertwined.

"That was very sweet of you, Grace," Joseph said.

"I'm glad you think so. You're not lying about enjoying the Marsala, are you?"

"Oh, please. If I thought it was a crap dinner, I wouldn't have gone for seconds, *dummy*."

Together we laughed, but it was almost painful to. Loaded with sauce and chicken, we lay there resting like two pigs in a pen.

I began thinking of how to persuade Mr. Winger, or Henry, to approach his contact at the paper. Surely he didn't have the time for a silly little assistant like me. Henry had published Nick's two novels back in the sixties, and when he heard of Nick's retirement from the academic realm, Henry was more than happy to add an experienced writer to his world. Henry did not expect a package deal though, with me as the added dependent. We'd spent maybe a total of an hour of speaking time since meeting a few weeks ago, and I wasn't even sure he remembered my name. My stomach gurgled at the thought, and with the Marsala.

Joseph sighed. "Just tell me, Grace. I can *feel* you overthinking."

There he went again, reading my mind. I said, "I have to convince Henry to convince his peers to publish me, sometime very soon."

Joseph squeezed my hand. "Just tell him the truth, Grace. Tell him what you've told me and Mr. Duncan."

"You mean *Nick*?" I teased.

He looked over to me and smirked. "On a first name basis. *Finally*."

I placed my head against his head and began to doze off.

"It'll be fine, Grace," he said through a yawn. "You'll find the words. You always do."

We all have a story.

Nick's mantra repeated in my mind over and over, until I gave in to the Marsala and fell asleep.

CHAPTER SEVEN

AT THAT TIME, Henry Winger was an older gentleman in his early fifties, and he towered over the whole of Philadelphia. He was a large man and almost always too busy to be bothered with anything other than his own business. If a mining tunnel caught fire below his feet and caused the earth to rip and rumble, he might have looked up from his desk for a split second, but he simply did not have time for more than that, nor did he ever entertain fools.

Why should he care about my story? What would it bring him, and what would it bring to the reader? These are the questions that Mr. Duncan—Nick—actually asked me in my senior year, and I replayed them in my head often.

For some reason, Nick arrived about an hour late that day, so I was left alone in the office with Henry. I sat at my desk with two cups of coffee prepared and the day's newspaper unfolded across the width of Nick's desk. I even arranged his pens in three parallel lines next to his piled inbox, the contents of which I straightened for him.

I had a feeling that his tardiness was my fault. Had I written a better article, maybe he wouldn't have had to spend so much time trying to make sense of it all.

"*Dammit*," I whispered to myself.

The door flew open to reveal Henry, his large hand on the doorknob. His eyes shot a laser beam at Nick's empty desk.

"Where *is* he?" he asked.

"I don't know," I answered, but it felt like a lie.

He glared at the tower of papers in Nick's inbox and then at me. "Would you step into my office, Grace?"

I nodded, swallowed the lump in my throat and followed. Henry's office was much larger than ours and was lined with bookshelves full of works that only he published—a sort of trophy case. There was a large spinning globe on his desk and a gold-plated vintage clock ticking away next to it. Beside the desk was a hand-carved wooden coat stand, and on the wall behind the desk, last but not least, hung a large portrait of Mark Twain in a chair in front of a bookshelf similar to Henry's, and wearing a white suit, as opposed to Henry's all-black attire. It was an enormously intimidating atmosphere.

He gestured for me to sit, and I did. I was facing him, and he watched as my eyes flicked back and forth between him and the painting.

"Do you know who that is?" he asked curiously.

I cleared my throat.

"It's Mark Twain, sir."

"Very good." He sat mirroring the posture that Twain embodied in the portrait.

He let out a long breath through his nose as he examined my face. I wondered what I was doing there. Was this his way of trying to get to know me? He hadn't said another word, so I crossed my legs and asked, "Do you have a favorite work of his?"

He pursed his lips and squinted. "Do *you*?"

"Yes," I answered swiftly. "*The Adventures of Huckleberry Finn.*"

"A popular read," he said.

"And *yours*?" I asked again.

He puffed his chest outward with a deep inhale. "I admire all of his works, hence why I purchased this art piece. It was about five thousand out of my pocket . . . worth *every* penny." His face curled into a devious smile, satisfied with an answer he knew I wouldn't expect.

I looked up into Twain's painted eyes. His expression suggested he was waiting on me, head tilting to the side and staring right back at me. I looked back to Henry and said, "A man cannot be comfortable without his own approval."

"Excuse me?" he asked, eyes narrowing.

"It's my favorite quote of Mark Twain."

"Is it now?" Henry cocked his head and deepened his brow, all the while trying to see what was going on inside my mind.

I informed him, "Every time I write something, I read over it when I've finished. Then I read it over once more, in case I missed something."

Henry lifted his back slightly off his chair, as if urging me to continue.

"Then, I read it out loud, to make sure that its tone makes sense to my ears the way it does to my eyes. If I don't like it, I try and try again, until I approve of it, just as Twain said. It means a lot to me."

"I see." He smoothed some stray hairs on his chin that only he could sense.

I felt the opportunity arise and silently drew in a breath. "Mr. Winger, *Henry* . . ." I started. "I've recently written something that I'd like you to consider."

He crossed his arms and closed the space between his back and the chair. "Oh *really?*"

"Yes. I've . . . written an exposé about the town of Centralia, in Columbia County. Have you heard of it?"

After a few seconds of contemplation, he lifted a finger onto the globe and spun it. "What, that tainted little town that was burnt to pieces?"

I gulped, stared down to my knotted hands, untied them, and

lifted my eyes. "Yes, sir. It was my hometown."

He observed my face, neck, and shoulders before arriving back to my eyes, and said nothing. I dragged in a small breath and said, "I'd like to inform Philadelphians about what it was like growing up there, everything from the accident to the smog, to everyday stuff, like getting groceries. I—"

"Wait, wait, wait," he mumbled.

I waited.

"Wasn't that town evacuated after the accident?"

I tried my best to remain expressionless. "Not *completely*."

A look of wonder sprouted on his face, and his mouth dropped open a bit. He rested both elbows on his desk and scooted to the edge of his seat.

"So . . . so what you're saying is, you lived in a ghost town?"

"In Centralia, sir, with my family."

I couldn't tell if he was puzzled or disgusted, or both, but my words had affected him, and it was blatant. He sucked in a large breath that almost emptied the room of air, but I was used to poor air quality anyway.

"You have my attention, Miss Grace."

I felt like I had unlocked the door to his mind and swallowed the key. I leaned forward and placed a hand on his desk, parallel to his elbow. "You're an avid reader, Henry."

"I am indeed," he boasted.

"But you've never heard much about my town, have you? I mean, you were under the impression that it was fully evacuated, until a moment ago."

"I was," he concurred.

I interlaced my fingers as if in prayer and set my hands on the edge of his desk. "Well, Henry, this is precisely *why* I wrote about it. Nobody has a clue about what really went on after the blast."

He leaned in a half inch more.

"And, I think that, as Mark Twain once said; 'Many a small thing has been made large by the right kind of advertising.'"

He raised his eyebrows, and I knew that he understood. For the first time, it felt like we were on the exact same page, *my* page. My crumpled, ink-stained page. The only sound now was the ticking of the clock.

Nick broke the silence, like a hurricane of a human, bursting through the door with his briefcase, his glasses slightly askew. It was very out of character for him. *Oh, no,* I thought. His coffee must be ice cold now.

Henry rose out of his seat, stomping out the door.

"Glad you could make it," Henry said to Nick without the slightest care for how condescending he sounded.

Nick stared, dumbfounded, and I left him to the mercy of Mark Twain. A fresh cup of coffee was seriously overdue for Nick, so I made myself useful.

After some time, Nick shuffled into our shared space and slapped a folder on my desk. "It's finished," he informed me, and then he slumped into his chair.

"Holy *hell*, Nick. You didn't have to do it all in one night. That's something, something . . . well, something that *I* would do!" I exclaimed.

He rubbed two small circles on his temples as I slid his replenished coffee mug closer to him. He took notice and lost himself in the round space inside the cup.

Finally, he said, "Did you speak with him?"

"With Henry?"

"Yes, yes. Who else? With *Henry*."

"Well, yes, I did."

"And?"

"And, I mentioned my piece. He . . . seems interested."

Nick threw his hands above his head and smirked. "Aha!"

It was my turn to be dumbfounded. "Nick, are you feeling ok?"

"All according to plan," he muttered whilst tapping his fingers against his desk.

I felt my face scrunch into a punctuation point. I was entirely perplexed.

"I perfected your piece," he said. "A full proofread, re-typed on pages unstained by ink, or coffee, or whatever happens to fall upon it when you write while *frustrated*."

"I appreciate that, Nick."

"It took all night, Grace. I mean, you emptied it out on paper in one night. Why shouldn't I do the same? But I knew I'd need an hour or so to make up for it in the morning."

"Like I said, I appreciate—"

"So, I thought it might be a good time for you to seize the moment."

I drew back into my chair. "You ... you *knew* this would happen?"

"I certainly hoped it would."

He tilted his mug all the way back to signal its emptying.

"And time is of the essence, is it not? You said it yourself, in your writing: 'Every day that goes by is another chance that Centralia may collapse completely.' You said it, Grace. Right there, on page four."

"Yes. Yes, I did."

"I knew you would take the chance. I knew the opportunity would arise to talk to Henry, and *bang*!" He smacked his hands together.

I took a deep breath and shook my head in disbelief. "This is ... one of the strangest mornings of my life," I said.

"And you're from *Centralia*," he added.

I rubbed my forehead and lifted my coffee mug. It was my turn to chase one back. Then I switched my attention to the folder and gently pulled out four pages. They were crisp, clean, and uniform.

"It's all there," he said. "I compressed it a little. Please, tell me what you think."

I followed the words of Mark Twain, and the words I had said earlier to Henry. I read it once, then once again, then out loud. It was *perfect*.

"Gosh, Nick. This is magnificent. You really . . . you really know how to make sense of my words."

Nick's face shone in agreement. "Well, I have graded a lot of your papers, Grace."

My once crumpled explosion of thought had been blessed by Nick's gracious edits. We exchanged smiles and then clinked our mugs together to celebrate our efforts.

Then, the door swung open as if by a large gust of wind; it was a bad day for the poor door hinges.

"Grace, a word," Henry demanded.

I nodded, quickly grabbing the folder and following him back to his office. I glanced back at Nick, who was still holding aloft his coffee mug, smiling at me.

Back inside his domain again, Henry sat in his chair and placed both of his hands on his desk, fingers spread so far apart I could see capillaries beneath the webbings.

"So, about this piece. How long is it?"

"An article's length."

"How many pages?"

"Four."

"And where is it?"

"Right here." I revealed it from my lap like magic. I slid it toward him and waited as he studied it, occasionally looking at me, while I sat there as still as a deer in headlights. Then he slapped it hard on his desk. It startled me, and I flinched.

"What do you expect me to do with this, Grace? Publish a fucking four-page novel?"

But I wasn't falling for this act. I remained calm and poised, deflecting his attempt to rattle me. "I heard that you have connections with *The Philadelphian.*"

He tutted and grabbed the folder again. "Let me guess, Nick told you this."

"Well, I've been . . . networking," I announced.

His fascinated expression conspired against his annoyed tone. I could read him like a book.

"Have you made edits?" he asked.

"A full proofread, by Nick, sir."

"*Right.* And you've gone over everything?"

"Read twice over, then spoken out loud."

"And do you *approve* of your work?"

"Yes, sir, I do. Do you?"

He paused and flicked his fingers through the pages. "I'll have to run it by some people," he replied.

I felt a smile trying to creep onto my lips, but I bit it back. I said, "Thank you for your time, Henry. I look forward to meeting with you again."

I stood up and stretched out my hand to shake his. He was taken aback by it, but slowly stood and ascended over me. He grabbed my hand and shook it firmly.

"My pleasure," he commented, eyes boring into mine.

I turned myself around and left his office with the broadest, most sincere smile I'd ever felt on my face. *I did it,* I thought. I'd submitted my first publishing query, albeit verbally, and I made it through to the other side. This is what that poor buck would have felt had he made it to the other side, too.

CHAPTER EIGHT

My brother, Sam, would have loved the city, and there was so much of it that I hadn't seen yet.

"Ready?" Joseph called.

"Let's go."

The summer sun hung high in the sky, so Joseph and I headed to a park in the city, a place that he is very fond of. "You're going to love it, Grace," he said.

It is a place called Wissahickon Valley Park, and it's one of the largest stretches of green in the city. Although the name was hard for me to say the first time, it's a very easygoing place to be. It boasts babbling brooks, shady woods, and vast meadows for miles and miles along a series of hiking trails. We decided to have a picnic together in one of the pastures and arrived at a gorgeous clearing in the center of it.

"My mother used to take me here," Joseph told me as he whipped open a checkered picnic blanket. "She'd make sandwiches and bake chocolate chip cookies, and we'd lie here and watch the clouds pass by after we had our fill." Joseph was beaming with delight.

"That sounds like such a happy memory, Joe."

On top of the blanket, I set down our picnic basket, which carried homemade pasta salad with heirloom tomatoes from our garden, two cheese-stuffed croissants, and, to my surprise, a half-size bottle of wine, a crisp sauvignon blanc.

"Is . . . is this allowed?"

Joseph snickered beside me. He was gazing up at the sun.

"This is my meadow today, so I'd say yes. May I?"

He swished away a piece of hair as I passed him the bottle. From his pants pocket, he pulled out an opener, twisted it hard into the cork and swiftly popped it off in an ostentatious act. Then, out of the bottom of the basket, he pulled out two red plastic cups, and I couldn't contain my laughter.

"What?" he prodded.

"Nothing, nothing. You were doing fine," I giggled.

"They were left over from Sully, in our dorm. I thought it would be nice."

I leaned toward him on the blanket and grabbed his hand. "It's perfect, Joe. Really."

A smile appeared on his sunlit face, and he poured two cups while I unwrapped the dishes. Around us were lines of white daisies in bloom and budding crocuses, dancing in a sea of wild meadow grass, shining green and lively under the midday sun. A breeze rolled through Joseph's hair; dark waves that were sporting a new, reddish-brown undertone in the gleaming daylight. Then the breeze carried on through the meadow, and the summer blooms waved hello to us.

"This was a lovely idea, Joe. Thank you for bringing me."

"See? I knew you would love it."

"It's no Nittany Hill, but it's a close second," I joked.

"Why don't we have a toast?" Joseph asked keenly.

We were the only ones around for what felt like miles, so we unashamedly held our cups high in the air above.

"To us," Joseph declared.

"And to the city," I added.

Sure, Sam would have loved the city, but this meadow belonged to Joe and me.

We took a sip from our cups and let out a nice long breath of air in unison.

"Sam and I used to go on picnics, too," I said.

"Did you?" he asked.

"We would all walk over to this old picnic table. It was actually beside Dad's old house." I took another sip and continued. "We would walk along the very edge of the road, hand in hand. Sam and I in the middle, Dad and Mom protecting us on the outside."

So they thought, I added to myself.

"What kind of food did you eat?" Joseph asked sweetly.

I had to think for a moment. I remembered our basket—an old, dingy little thing with broken weave. It was never full to the top with homemade salads, fresh garden veggies, or sweet chocolate chip cookies like Joseph had eaten on his picnics.

"Bread, mostly."

Joseph raised his eyebrows. I could tell he was thinking of something nice to say.

I added, "Sometimes we would have pie, though, if the shop had any in the window."

"*Cherry* pie?"

"Of course."

I looked into my cup and took a very large gulp from it, spilling a drop down my chin.

"Easy there," Joseph teased.

My stomach fluttered at the drink, and a sense of euphoria came over me. I leaned back onto my elbows, looking up into the clouds. Joseph mirrored my body, and stared upward with me.

"Any word from Henry yet?" Joseph asked.

I sighed, "No, not yet."

I had been waiting weeks for Henry's reply and was beginning to wonder if he was just gassing me up about sending my work to one of his contacts.

Joseph moved off his elbows and lay flat against the blanket. "I see . . . a dog." He pointed to a cumulus cloud above. Joseph was sweet, and I think that he knew I didn't want to think about the article at that time.

It was there, alright. "I see it, too," I replied, lying down beside him, and searching for a cloud of my own.

"I see . . . a rabbit."

Joseph paused as he searched for another.

"Hmm. I see a goldfish." Joseph pointed to a stratus cloud, and there it was, fins and all.

I turned my eyes closer to the sun, squinting them hard against its blinding light as I focused on another cloud. I lifted up a hand to shield my eyes, and then made my discovery below my pinky finger.

"I see . . . a newspaper!" I pointed out a cloud to the right, long and rectangular with stripes of stratus clouds running through it as headlines. When I turned my head, I saw him staring at my face.

"What?" I asked. He was looking at me, smiling that sweet smile he wears.

"I see . . ." His eyes were tracing every corner of my face, and I couldn't help but smile. "I see the most beautiful girl in the world."

In the bright summer sun, there was no hiding from the blush that grew on my cheeks. Joseph slowly rose up to lean over me and kiss me softly on the lips. It was as intoxicating as the summer sun, and the drink in my cup.

The kiss was everlasting, and the meadow hushed in a symphony of rustled petals, whispering their secrets to each other in a love language of their own. It was the perfect orchestra for our moment, a moment that we hung onto tenderly as we basked in the warm rays that undulated down upon us. Our lips parted, and when our eyes met again, I said, "I only see you."

It was an absolutely, unreservedly, categorically perfect day.

CHAPTER NINE

I STOPPED BY HENRY'S DESK every morning, to his annoyance, waiting for his reply. I'd been shushed away too many times and had been tapping my pen against my leg so much it was starting to leave a mark. Weeks went by, until finally Henry called me into his office with the news.

"Sit down, Grace."

I sat. Henry glanced at the clock, waiting for the second hand to circle back to twelve, and then began.

"Grace . . ."

I closed my eyes for a moment.

"*The Philadelphian* is interested in your story."

My eyes sprung open, and I could almost feel my pupils dilating.

"They're offering a full page, the second page after the fold. September's issue, no photographs."

That was just two weeks away.

"Oh, thank you. Thank you, Henry!" I rose up from my seat.

"But, Grace . . ."

I stopped in my place.

"They need a title."

Damn, I had been so wrapped up in it that I hadn't even thought about a title. I returned to my seat and wondered.

"*Now*, Grace. They need it *now*." He picked up his phone and held it to his face to further demonstrate the importance of it.

I remembered what he had called it, the first time I mentioned it to him. He said: *What, that tainted little town?*

"The Tainted Town," I whispered.

"What was that?"

"The Tainted Town. That's the title."

He clicked open a pen and wrote it down on a notepad beside the phone. "Right," he responded.

Phone pressed against his ear and shoulder, he waved one hand at me to exit his office while he dialed a number with the other. "Er, thank you, Grace," he said.

I nodded, shut the door behind me, accepted the title that I'd chosen, and went back to work.

CHAPTER TEN

I KNEW THAT I WOULDN'T catch any sleep on the night of August 31. I was far too excited.

I took the bus to get to work early, wanting to be the first to retrieve the newspaper. But to my surprise, there was nothing on the doorstep when I had arrived. I rubbed my eyes, thinking maybe my lack of sleep had blurred my vision, but still nothing. Inside I didn't see any light shining on Nick's desk, and I didn't see Nick, either.

When I walked in, Henry's office door was open just a crack with a bright yellow glow pouring out of it. I could hear murmuring coming from within, so I slowly walked to his door and gave it a little push.

"Ah, there you are!" Nick exclaimed, throwing an arm around my shoulder. "Hail!"

He had made *me* a cup of coffee, *just* the way I liked it: one sugar, hold the cream. Meanwhile, Henry unfolded the newspaper in front me, and I stood before it, my eyes shimmering like embers at the words. There was the headline:. *The Tainted Town: The true story about the town of Centralia.*

It was all mine, and all of Philadelphia's at the same time. I envisioned the paper making its way onto the city's doorsteps, through mailboxes, and landing on desks, delivered to executives and construction workers, to mothers and teachers, to accountants and lawyers and shopkeepers. I even pictured a loyal Fido taking it to his owner to read over breakfast. They were all reading *my* work at the *exact* same time, and it was overwhelming me in the best way possible.

"Congratulations, Grace, on your *first* publication," Nick rejoiced.

"Good work, Miss Grace," Henry said, respectfully.

"Thank you, to both of you; I *literally* could not have done it without you."

"Oh, we know," Henry added before being quieted by Nick's scolding glare.

I knew it, too. I had the luck of being in the right place at the right time with the right people. No matter how unfriendly Henry could be at times, he had done me a good turn, and I respected the hell out of him for it. I heard Henry's words but took them as praise. Then, I looked over at Mark Twain's portrait, gave him a nod, and I swear I saw him wink at me.

The weekend after my story got out, Joseph, Emilia, and Richard conspired to throw a party at the house to celebrate. I thought it was all a little extreme, but apparently word of my article had gotten around the city in less than a week. A group of their friends were interested in speaking with me about the article, and meeting me, too. It wasn't the reaction I had expected.

"Oh, it'll be good for you, dear. Come, sit, eat, and mingle with everyone," Emilia advised. "You've written your words. Now, you must *use* them."

Emilia was right, and this gathering would only bring more attention to the issues in Centralia. So, who was I to say no to a house full of people who'd like a share of my time? Joseph had even invited Sully to show up, who'd been busy practicing after being drafted for the Baltimore Ravens awhile back. It was unbelievable, really, just how many people could fit into one house.

Dad and my mother had been invited, of course, but my mother hadn't been feeling well, so they did not attend. I didn't really pay any mind to it; sometimes Centralia makes you feel ill, with its toxic air. I understood it, and it's not like I was expecting my mother to celebrate my article that completely denounced her homeland.

Emilia had bought for me a beautiful floor-length red dress to match the pumps I'd had for years. It was all too much for me to handle, but for the sake of gratitude and to keep up appearances, I slipped the dress on, twirled my hair up in a clip, and swiped over my pout with some red lipstick. I was putting on airs for a crowd of interested Philadelphians. Staring at my reflection in the bedroom mirror, I barely recognized the woman peering back at me.

"*Wow.*" Joseph appeared out of nowhere, while I was stalling going downstairs.

I gasped in a fright, and he playfully gasped, too.

"Emilia is so sweet. She didn't have to do this," I said.

"It was actually my idea," he bragged.

I raised an eyebrow at him.

"The dress, I mean," he added with a grin.

"Oh. Oh, I see," I said, sweeping my dress down my sides.

He walked over to me, dressed in a gray suit and red tie, looking more dapper than ever before. I pulled him in by the tie and planted a kiss on his lips. He swung his arm up, and I hooked my arm through it.

"Ready to head down?"

"No," I admitted.

But he nudged me anyway, taking one last look at us in the mirror before heading down the stairs into the throng of people.

The large chandelier shimmered above us, and the first person I saw was Sully, who waited at the edge of the stairs, and scooped me up for a big hug.

"Sully!" I shouted.

"Hey there, big shot!"

"Oh, you made it! How have you been?"

"As good as it can get, *baby*!" He howled, before carefully setting me back onto my heels.

"Sully, did you read my piece?"

"I *did* . . . only about half an hour ago," he admitted. "Thanks to your man, here."

I looked over to Joseph, and he gave a bashful smile and shrugged. Around the corner I could hear the muttering of strangers. I straightened my posture and locked arms with Joseph once again, moving toward the crowd, Sully following, as if waiting for us to throw him the ball.

Throughout the night, I was approached by a plethora of locals, just as I had envisioned. Those executives and teachers and hims and hers, friends of Emilia and Richard, and friends of their friends. One of them was a local news reporter, who asked *me* for a quick interview for Studio 7 News! She slipped me a business card after a brief discussion, during which she used the word "scoop" a handful of times, before I was pulled away again by the next eager Philadelphian.

"Oh, Grace, please tell me more about the accident."

"Grace, so nice to meet you. Tell me about the fire; where were you?"

"How many people are still living there today? How's your family doing over there, Grace?"

"Grace! Over here!"

Back and forth, left and right, around the foyer and the large living room, I chatted to jabbering folk while others were sipping cocktails in the kitchen and dining area. I was feeling very out of place. Joseph and Sully stuck by my side the entire time as my loyal companions.

"Yeesh," Sully groaned. "They're like barking dogs." He let out a quiet howl only Joseph and I could hear. "Awoo awoo!" We all snickered at that, and I was relieved by it. It was so nice to hear him say what I had been thinking.

"Don't they know they're in the presence of three *lions*?" Sully asked.

I'd only then noticed that he was wearing a suit with the colors of our alma mater. To everyone else, he was the running back for the Ravens—tall, fit, and dressed in blue and white. To us, he was our college pal, our pride and joy, appropriately adorned in our Nittany navy and white. We exchanged a trio of proud glances and brightened ourselves up to the onlookers. We were in our own leonine class. How good it felt to be back with my pride again, us three Nittany lions in a house full of dogs, letting each one of them close enough, if they dare, one by one, to sniff out the mighty lioness.

I explained Centralia to these people to the best of my ability, answering their questions with solid facts, as well as my personal accounts. For the whole night, I was catering to every single suit and tie, every gown, every martini and glass of scotch. I didn't shy away, didn't offend anyone or trip over my words. It was a whole new dimension that I was maneuvering through, a dimension of narcissism that I couldn't understand until it all wrapped up, and things began to feel normal again. Around midnight, the partygoers, many whose names I wouldn't remember, had all left. Sully had said goodbye as well—more of a "see you cats later."

The entire house, once bursting with sophisticated chatter and laughter, had fallen silent. I found myself in the garden, alone, taking in a much-needed breath of fresh September air. I thought about the reporter, and how she had repeated herself three times in a row about how important it would be to give her a call. I still had her card in my hand and traced over her name with my finger.

Kelly O'Connor – Journalist, Studio 7 News.

God, I thought, *can I really do this?* Should I continue to inform the public, and at what cost? What could I *really* achieve by going on air, and what the hell would I even *say*? I was interrupted by Joseph, who crept up behind me and placed a hand on my neck.

"*Oh*! It's you."

"Sorry, I didn't mean to scare you."

"I'm not afraid," I protested.

He smiled at me.

"I didn't say you were. Haven't we had this conversation before?"

"When we met?"

We laughed, and he stood behind me, wrapping his arms around mine.

"You did so well tonight, Grace. Really, I can't believe it. And you look . . ."

I felt my face turn the hue of my dress. "Oh, *stop*," I teased.

We gazed up at the moon together, full and bright in a cloudless sky, beaming down like a spotlight.

"You know, I really think you should contact that reporter," Joseph commented. "Who knows? You could have a whole list of publications under your belt by the year's end."

It was a heavenly thought.

"I know. I think so, too," I agreed.

It was an accomplishment, for sure, something that I could add to a resume, right under my degree. That's what I'd wanted, that and a chance to tell Pennsylvania about its long-hidden secret. I looked down to my feet and pondered for a moment, imagining myself sitting next to Kelly on some lovely, bright blue couch while she gabbed away about my article on live television. I smiled to myself before Joseph caught a glimpse of it, and then a smile ripened on his face to match. I brought my eyes back up to the moon and noticed that a large gray cloud had appeared out of nowhere, consuming the moon entirely and darkening our faces.

I heard the large glass doors to the garden open up and there stood Richard.

"Grace?" he said.

He was a dark silhouette in front of me, but I could see that his face was sunken in, and his hands were shaking noticeably. I took a step forward.

"What is it?" I asked.

"Grace, it's your mother. She . . ."

"She's what?"

I took another step forward.

"She—she's done something," Richard muttered through a broken voice.

He wouldn't look me in the eyes, and I couldn't understand the countenance he wore. Behind him, I could see Emilia in the kitchen holding the phone to her ear and pressing her hand over her mouth. She turned to look at me with tears in her eyes.

"*What?* What has she done?" I shouted.

Richard lifted his head up to approach mine.

"She's gone, Grace."

I felt the darkness of the night closing in around me. It forced its way through me, wrapping around my lungs, and ringing them out of air. The gray cloud circled around my head in a fog, and my hands grew so numb that I couldn't feel them picking away at my scar. My stomach and heart writhed around in my chest, pressing against each other to become one aching organ. A wave of heat prickled across every inch of my skin only to be followed mercilessly by beads of cold sweat. In the background I could see Emilia still clutching the phone. She looked like she was miles away.

I stumbled in my mother's heels as I ran to the phone in what felt like a never-ending mining tunnel. I grabbed the phone from Emilia's hand and held it to my ear. There I could only hear the awful sounds of Dad's sobs and breaths, and then I heard what sounded like rushing water in my ears. As the dark waves crashed inside of my head, I fell down hard onto my knees. I felt the phone slip out of my hand, and my head colliding with the cold kitchen floor, my vision fading to black.

When I woke up, I was in the bedroom, lying on my pillow. Joseph was beside me, watching over me and stroking my hair.

"Is this a dream?" I whispered, desperately.

But he just stared at me, like I was a broken clock that was still trying to tell the time.

"No, Grace. I'm here," he said.

"Dad?" I croaked.

"Emilia is talking to him. He's ok, Grace. Don't worry," Joseph said.

The rushing water in my ears had made its way to my eyes and turned into my tears. My mother had taken her life that night.

She was becoming increasingly distant and delirious over the last month, and Bill hadn't mentioned it so as not to worry me. When the pharmacy closed earlier in the year, she had kept a secret stash of quaaludes tucked away under a floorboard. She tried her hardest to quit, but none of us had ever taken her dependency seriously enough. It was just something that she had always done, since my birth father had passed. I'd see her try to hide it, pretending to wipe her nose as she tossed a little white pill into her mouth, followed by a sip of wine. We all had our coping methods in Centralia. I smoked my cigarettes; Bill had his infatuation with my mother; my mother had her pills. I never, *ever* thought that she would use them as a weapon against herself, but maybe I should have. Bill swore he had no idea she kept them.

She'd mixed them with an old bottle of whiskey that belonged to my birth father, swallowed them all in secret, crawled into bed like normal, and left a note underneath her pillow.

I love you two with all my heart. Please understand and let me be at peace. Let me be with Sam.

I couldn't eat. I couldn't move. I couldn't talk. Bill was all alone, and he kept calling. But I couldn't talk. I couldn't eat. I couldn't move. I just wanted my mother back. I just wanted to sleep.

———————

I didn't want Joseph to take time off work. It would only make me feel like more of a liability, and I don't think there was much that he could do to fix me anyway. I just lay there, in bed, in my madness, navigating through the underground tunnels in my head, trying to find where it all went wrong.

The one time my mother had made it to Philadelphia to visit me, she was glowing in the city's lights. She was happy, gleeful, and sometimes she'd be grinning wide in little, fleeting moments that I was lucky enough to catch. I remember how tired she was after our day trip. Her feet ached, and the Italian food did not sit right in her stomach that night. She and Bill stayed with us before leaving in the morning, set up on the sofa bed together. I overheard a moment of the two of them after we had said our goodnights. I was lingering in the hallway, listening to them whisper like happy little children. Bill was rubbing her feet, and she was leaning back on the bed. She let out little groans as he massaged the soreness away.

"Goodness," she said, "I haven't walked this much in years."

"I'm surprised they didn't fall right off of your legs," Bill teased.

She laughed. It was a quiet, modest laugh, and I could hear an undertone beneath it. She was still out of her element in the exceedingly large living room with bright, contemporary furniture. It all seemed to astound her as she peered around the room. I heard them settle under the covers.

"What are you thinking about?" Bill asked.

"Oh, oh nothing."

"Oh, come on, Rita. What is it?"

"It's—I feel . . ."

"You feel . . .?"

"I . . . I hope I haven't been a distraction for everyone today. I *know* what they must think of me, and—"

"Think of you? Oh, no, dear, you've got it all wrong. You—"

"Bill, it's alright."

He released a heartfelt sigh, and I remained a voiceless ghost hanging around the corner.

"It's a *wonderful* place, Philadelphia. It's everything that I ever hoped for. But, I still—I still feel like . . ."

There was silence, and I debated revealing myself to them before she spoke again.

"I don't belong here, Bill."

I shook my head at that. *No,* I thought, I had heard enough. So, I disappeared into the foyer, making my way up the stairs to bed. I had taken her words with a pinch of salt. At the time, I was so certain that she was wrong, that she just needed to adjust to her surroundings. It would grow on her, I thought, just as it had grown on me.

Could it have been her aching feet that dissuaded her to return? Or perhaps the bright sunlight, or the way the furniture looked? There had to be something, one final straw that pulled her back into the belly of the beast. I thought that she would be ready to leave Centralia, that I could make her ready. How wrong I was. My mother was a moth drawn to the light only to be burned by it.

It is always the same, just as she wrote in her letter.

Let me be with Sam.

It's as if her spirit were tied to the land, intertwined with Sam's and my father's. I couldn't save her. I couldn't save any of them. So, why did I believe so surely that I could? How could I have been so *stupid?* Maybe it's from all the books that I read growing up, all the fairytales and mythology leading me to believe that there could *truly* be a happy ending for us.

Joseph interrupted these thoughts, which I had so often, and could last for hours. But he was there by my side for these hours, holding my hand tightly and erasing my tears, when he would have normally been hard at work. He insisted he stayed here with me, and I loved him for it, surely.

In a way, I suppose that it was better to feel like a burden than to feel like a broken record, re-playing the thoughts in my mind over and over again until my exhaustion gave way, sending me into another nightmare, which Joseph pulled me out of, too. I didn't want to be a burden, but I am so thankful to have had him there.

CHAPTER ELEVEN

EVERY NIGHT I SAW HER FACE in my dreams. She was standing there in that red dress that she wore in Philadelphia, and every day I flipped back and forth through our only album of photos of us together. She was happy then. She looked *so* happy. She deserved so much better than the life she lived. All I wanted was to show her that she could leave it all behind. But I was wrong.

Two weeks to the day, there were fresh-cut daisies in a vase next to a pitcher of ice water by my bed, along with a slice of cherry pie, a copy of Nick's mystery novel, and a letter from Sully offering his regards, with a touch of his dark humor.

Two weeks since I'd left the room, and two weeks since my last cup of coffee. So, I listened to my stomach instead of my head and got out of bed to go to the kitchen. On my way out, I passed myself in the mirror. I was a completely different person than the last time I had looked. Through the glass, a *ghost* was staring back at me. She imitated my posture and had puffy, bloodshot eyes surrounded by dark circles, and dry, cracked lips that were sealed shut, and protruding clavicles splaying out along her neckline. A bony, gnarled hand curled upward to brush away a matted piece of once-blonde hair turned brown with sweat and tears. I was deeply afraid of her, and she wouldn't stop staring at me. I looked away from her, and I think she looked away, too, and then made my way down to the brightly lit kitchen.

"Grace! Here," Joseph said, walking up to me and offering me his arm. "How are you, darling?"

"I'm ok," I squeaked through my lips. My voice was raspy, thick, and out of practice.

Richard and Emilia were standing beside him, and it was obvious to me that I had interrupted a conversation about me. Richard grabbed a mug from a cabinet and swiftly poured some coffee into it. He must've picked up on my craving for it, the way that Joseph read my mind sometimes. I looked around the kitchen, so pristine and shiny, adjusting my eyes to the room like it was my first time inside, when my eyes met the phone again. Instantly, I wanted to drop down and cry, but I noticed that there was that reporter's card stuck to it with tape, staring at me in the face.

Kelly O'Connor, the journalist for Studio 7 news. *"Remember, Grace, my number is the main line. I'll be waiting for your call,"* she said.

I didn't hesitate any longer. I picked up the phone and dialed the main line. I could feel Joseph, Richard, and Emilia's unsure eyes on me, so I turned to the side. After a few rings, a peppy Kelly O'Connor answered.

I cleared my throat.

"Hi Kelly, this is Grace. We spoke a few weeks ago, I—*ahem* . . ."

"Yes, yes, Grace! Oh, thank goodness you called. We've been waiting for ya! Tell us, did you decide on that interview? It's not too late, you know."

I felt out of breath just listening to her chatter. "Yes, Kelly. I've decided. I'm ready."

"Oh, super! Just super! Here, let me put you on a brief hold while my assistant handles the booking. This is great, Grace. Just a sec!"

I cleared my throat again and waited patiently for her assistant, almost as bubbly as she was, and quickly set a time and date for September 29, five days away.

When I ended the call, I turned to Richard. He passed me the coffee mug. I held it in my hands, absorbing its warmth. Then I closed my eyes and took my first sip of it. Swirls of hazelnut and cocoa danced around my mouth in a parade of boldness and bitterness, with just a hint of delicate sweetness as the cherry on top. I felt its warmth trickle down the back of my throat and pour into my stomach, warming me up from the inside out. I inhaled its aroma through my nose and exhaled a wave of steam past my lips. Almost instantly my stomach curdled at it, and my eyes vibrated from the rush of caffeine. When I opened them, Joseph was standing in front of me, smiling sweetly.

I mirrored him and flashed my first smile in two weeks. Two weeks of fourteen-hour sleeps, tear-stained pillowcases, matted hair, and a dehydrated mind and body. Two weeks of refusing meals or condolences, and two weeks of crying myself to sleep. It felt like a lifetime of misery, and I imagined it had to be what my mother must have felt in the days leading to her death. I decided that I wanted to end my misery, too, but not like her.

CHAPTER TWELVE

I ADMIT THAT I WAS UNWELL. I felt like I was just sort of floating through time. I was receiving calls from Kelly with a list of questions that I had to come up with answers to in the next few days. Bill had been calling, too.

In my mental absence, and Bill's despair, Richard and Emilia had sorted out how to deal with my mother's passing. Columbia County had to send a coroner over to claim her body, and she was sent a few towns away to Farrow Funeral Directors for cremation.

Bill refused any plans for a funeral, but he did accept some help that was offered. He quickly decided that there was nothing left for him in Centralia. Richard had been answering his phone calls and jumped to his aid, working hard to sort out a job with one of his many connections. Construction was flourishing in the city, so it wasn't too long before he found Bill some manual labor to start him off.

All three of them had been speaking to Bill every day, making sure that he knew he had options, making sure that he was in his right mind, and updating him about how I was doing. I should have been stronger. I should have called earlier. Bill needed me.

I set down the coffee mug and collected my thoughts. My next phone call was to speak to Bill, and for this call, they left me in the kitchen. I was alone, and I was so nervous to speak to him. But the stir of nerves in my belly gave me a similar feeling, like happy little butterflies in my stomach, so I took a deep breath, in through the nose and out through the mouth, and dialed his number. The phone did not ring even once; Bill picked up straightaway.

"Grace?"

"Dad," I whispered.

"Oh, *Grace*. Thank God, Grace."

I instantly cracked at the sound of his voice. "Dad. Dad. I'm sorry. I'm so sorry, Dad. I love you. I love you, so much," I sobbed.

"Grace, it's ok. It's ok, I know. *I know*, kiddo. I love you too."

"I should have been there!' I cried.

"*No*, Grace, you shouldn't. *We* shouldn't."

I tried so hard to breathe normally, but I couldn't relax.

"Grace, have you spoken to Joseph?"

"What?" I asked.

"It's over, Grace. I'm—I'm done with this place. There's nothing. Nothing left." He sniffled. "I'm coming to you, kiddo. I'm leaving this, this, this damned place for *good*."

Richard and Emilia agreed with Bill. There really was nothing left for him there, and he would *not* end up like that poor buck. He quit his job, packed up some bags, threw them into his car, and decided to leave it all behind. My mother was the glue, keeping the house standing and keeping Bill next to her while she lost her mind. I imagine that as soon as he took his final step out that crooked door on that crooked foundation, that it would all crumble. Crumble and sink down into the earth forever. To hell with it all.

I had so much preparation to do, for the interview, and for Bill. He wasn't quite ready to leave the house yet, having to pack everything all by himself. So, I used the time to ready myself for the interview. I had taken my first shower in weeks, and I could barely stand up in it. The heat went right through me. Joseph waited for me outside the door and walked me back to the bedroom to brush out my hair.

"You don't have to do this, Joe."

"I know."

But he insisted, and began brushing away at my tangled mane, gentle as can be. I closed my eyes and felt tears well up. He helped me practice for the interview as he ran the brush through my hair, reciting the questions Kelly had proposed for me as my strands slowly came back to life. I thought about my mother, and how she deserved a proper send off. I thought of Sam and my father, too. It exhausted me, but Joseph's touch eased my pain as he brushed away each intrusive thought. The questions asked were already answered in my article, and my answers were memories that already played in my head every day. I tried not to overthink them all with so much on my mind to begin with. Joseph smoothed his last strand and stopped brushing.

"Go look."

He pointed to the mirror, and I shifted off the bed. I stood in front of the glass. The ghost from before wasn't there anymore.

Richard and Emilia had offered Bill residence in our home, but he denied their offer. He was too proud and didn't want to encumber them. I shared these traits with him, adopting them from him the way that he adopted me as his daughter. I had circled so many apartment listings in the newspaper the past few months, and Richard had saved them all. I'm glad he was being proactive while I was falling apart. Now I was slowly trying to rebuild myself as my family was evolving yet again.

Richard and Emilia cared so, so much about me, and about Bill. They found him a small space to migrate to, where he could be close to us and his new job, building and developing the city. Sam would have been so proud of him. Richard and Emilia had saved yet another Centralian from being buried in the ashes like so much of that tainted town, that wretched little place that was burnt to pieces, like Henry had said.

I was closing in on the end of my bereavement leave, while also closing in on my interview and Bill's arrival. "Take as much time as you need," Nick had offered. But like Bill, I was too proud and didn't want to be a burden. Getting back onto my feet after a fall was something I'd been doing since I fell on the road when the accident with Sam happened.

Sleeping all day and wasting away is just what my mother had done, and I could not, and would not repeat the cycle. I wouldn't turn to drugs or drink. I would not give into delirium, hard as it was to ignore the intrusive thoughts. I wanted to be stronger than that, and sulking around wasn't productive at all. I had a story to tell to the entire city of Philadelphia on live television. I had work to do, hair to wash, interview answers to practice, and a father to love. I had a town that I could truly leave behind now if I wanted, to never think of again, to let go of entirely. It couldn't hurt me anymore.

Or I could keep it. I could keep Centralia in my mind, and I could use it. I could actually *do* something about it. What that was, though, I was not entirely sure yet.

CHAPTER THIRTEEN

"COMMUNICATION POINTS" were what Kelly called them. There are four questions expected to be answered along with a full minute of airtime to discuss the topic freely, where Camera Two would be zoomed in on me from the waist up.

"Remember, keep it simple. Summarize it, and then build on it a bit," Kelly informed me confidently.

I was at the city's center in an area called Fairmount, at Studio 7. I arrived promptly at seven o'clock in the morning, dressed in my Sunday best—a dark purple dress that was laid out the night before, and my mother's red pumps on my feet again. My hair was brushed out, by myself.

Joseph was kind enough to drive me, and we pulled into our reserved parking spot, marked *Kelly – Guest*.

"Am I allowed to enter?" he asked.

"Honestly, I have no idea."

He was staring at me with puppy dog eyes.

"What is it?"

"You just . . . you look beautiful."

I felt my cheeks flood crimson.

"You're going to do great, Grace. Look at you."

I giggled and he looked at me like the sunrise was pouring out of me.

"I love you," he added.

"Always," I returned.

He pulled me in for a kiss on the forehead and opened the car door from the inside for me.

When I entered the building, that bubbly receptionist motioned for me to head down the hall to my right and follow the people, lights, and cables.

"Oh, super! There you are." Kelly beamed. "Right over here, Grace."

She was dressed in a navy-blue pantsuit with shoulder pads stacked high, and maybe three quarters of a can of Aqua Net keeping her strawberry-blonde hair in place. She had a full face of make-up on with a deep red blush almost completely disguising her freckles. She looked like a business Barbie doll and had the personality to match. I followed her into the dressing room where a make-up artist and a technician were.

"Coffee?" she offered.

"Oh, thank you."

"Here ya go!"

Kelly snapped her polished finger and summoned a young guy who appeared from thin air and positioned a hot paper cup in my hand. I thanked him and took a sip. It was black coffee, and very, very strong. It certainly explained why everyone was so peppy there. When I turned back around, he was gone.

"So, how are you feeling? Ready to tell the world?" Kelly asked.

I wasn't expecting the question, but still answered firmly. "Absolutely."

"That's the spirit!" she exclaimed, throwing her hand into a fist.

A young woman with an equally painted face appeared in front of me with a make-up brush and palette and began patting color onto my cheeks.

"Don't mind me, sugar," she said sweetly but surely.

I was feeling out of place again.

"Now, do you have everything prepared? Been practicing what you want to say?"

Unable to speak with a pencil being pressed to my lip, I mumbled, "Mhmm."

"Now, let me just go over a few things. Under no circumstances will there be *any* swearing. *No* gum chewing, *no* mumbling and *no* unbecoming posture. We will have you sitting slightly turned toward me and slightly toward the camera."

She went on and on, speaking like a speeding bullet. *Nerves of steel* this and *big smile* that. It was a boat load of tips and rules that mostly went over my head. I wondered if she had read my piece at all. I'd been living my entire life constantly on edge, literally dodging death until I was eighteen years old. I think I could handle a five-minute interview.

I had typed up my responses the night before so that Kelly could go over and approve of them. I took my time on them, but she took only a second to skim over them in a process not at all comparable to my Twain-inspired review technique.

"Ok, ok, super. Now, remember, this is live television, sweetie. Make it count!"

A piercing bell rang across the studio, signaling the ten-minute point. I was told to stand up, and a faceless technician began to wire me up with a microphone. Pairs of hands were manipulating my body like puppeteers, swishing my hair around and taping equipment to my back. After all of that, I was deemed presentable and escorted to the newsroom.

An ugly, curved, bright orange couch without any pillows was to be my seat, about three feet apart from Kelly. I took my seat and was offered some more of that wickedly strong coffee in a large mug with that same bright orange "7" shamelessly slapped on either side of it. I obliged, took a scorching sip of it, and placed it on a tiny end table to my right.

Kelly took her seat to my left while the make-up artist arrived to apply the final touches to my cheeks. She flicked away stray hairs bordering my face and straightened my back a bit with the palm of her hand.

Three blinding lights shone above and in front of us while two cameras stood below them. There were about twelve people sharing the room with us, making it about as warm as Centralia itself. A man clicked on a teleprompter in front of Kelly and the one-minute bell let out its brain-rattling call.

Kelly licked her lips and flipped her hair back. I positioned myself slightly off center to Kelly, half facing the camera as instructed, which felt very unnatural and silly. I crossed my legs and interlaced my fingers.

"Ready?" Kelly asked.

I drew in a hot breath and nodded. Maybe it was the coffee, but suddenly I felt like I was going to freeze up. A technician held up his hands and counted down on his fingers; while I counted the ways I could jump up and run out.

Five, four, three, two . . .

"Good morning, Philadelphia. Kelly O'Connor here to start your day off with a scoop! I'm joined today by a courageous young woman, Grace, to talk to you about the widely unknown tragedy that happened in her hometown of Centralia, Pennsylvania. How are you doing today, Grace?"

I silently cleared my throat behind a *big smile.*

"Good morning, Kelly. I'm doing just fine, thank you for having me."

"Well, thank you for coming. Now, first of all, why don't you tell us a little about Centralia?"

I tried hard not to look at the camera and said, "Well, it's a small town in southeast Columbia County, and it's a coal mining town. I grew up there with my mother, father, and younger brother, Sam."

"That's right. For those of you who haven't read about it in *The Philadelphian*, Centralia suffered a coal mine explosion eighteen years ago, which severely crippled the town and its resources. Most people believed the town to be fully evacuated after such an extreme event, with the fire still burning underground today. But . . . that's not quite the case. Tell us more about what it was like for you to grow up in such a devastated atmosphere."

I took a small pause at the loaded statement and then began my discourse.

"To be quite honest, Kelly, I'm not sure how I made it out alive. My father was killed in the initial explosion. We lost schools, our only hospital, our post office, and dozens of homes. Years later, my younger brother fell through a crack in the road, and I lost him, too."

Things were taking a darker turn; much less bubbly and bright then Kelly seemed to appreciate.

Nevertheless, I continued. "Everywhere I went I could smell the fire. The saner town folk moved away, but a couple hundred stuck around."

I was interrupted by Kelly's infectious energy. "Yes, research shows that only fifty residents remain in Centralia today. So, what would you have to say to them now, Grace?"

I had to think for a moment, and I broke one of her rules by staring into the camera. "I would say . . . I would say . . ."

Kelly was beaming her bright eyes straight into my soul with irritated anticipation.

"To leave while you still can. Come to your senses. The fire still burns day and night below your homes. Do it for the children, like me, who barely made it out alive. Or do it for the children who died, like my brother Sam."

There was an uneasy pause that took over the studio, but Kelly, being the professional that she is, very quickly lightened the mood with a host of compliments about my bravery, and how my words moved her and all of Philadelphia.

"I can't imagine what that must have been like, Grace. Now, you are a graduate of Pennsylvania State, and you're living in Philadelphia working for a publishing company, is that correct?"

How easy it was for her to ask all those questions with little to no reaction amazed me.

"Yes, it is. I graduated this May, and I am now working for Stark Publishing Company."

I could picture Henry stirring in his office at the sound of his company making the news.

"Well, that's wonderful news. Such a magnificent turnaround for you, and we're happy to have you in our city."

I presented the studio with a less inviting smile, but stayed true to myself.

"It is such an important story to be told, Grace. Thank you so much for coming on."

"Thank you, Kelly."

"To find out more about Centralia you can still purchase a copy of *The Philadelphian*'s earlier release this month for a limited time only to explore Centralia through Grace's words. We'll be back after this."

The studio bell rang, employees rushed around, and the interview closed. I exhaled and looked down at my hands, opening them up to reveal a streak of blood. I had nervously picked away at my old scar, reopening those wounds that I had been trying to run away from. I wondered if the blood had been broadcast.

Although the interview did not go as I had imagined, I'm glad I said what I did. Kelly didn't seem very pleased with my answers, going off from her pretentious guidelines, but I was satisfied with the outcome. I didn't get my minute-long platform, but it was worth the short yet bold responses, without sugar-coating the story of my life.

I was quickly de-wired and released from the press without any send-off from Kelly. She was either busy, uninterested, or both. It didn't bother me. She had her piece, and I had my soapbox. I reached the exit and found Joseph outside at the guest parking spot, leaning against his car, looking like a modern James Dean.

"I'm driving," I declared.

"Uh, *what?*" he asked defiantly.

I was still living in my moment of confidence, my five minutes of fame. He shot me a look that read "no way," and I returned a look that said, "yes way." I had already broken the studio's rules today and was feeling a little dangerous. An unlicensed joy ride, albeit just over ten minutes from the house, was calling my name. Joseph scratched at his head and sighed.

"Grace, if you kill us, I swear I'll avoid you in heaven."

"If I kill us, I'll be in hell," I snickered.

He shook his head and tossed me the keys. We swapped seats, and I enjoyed seeing him sit on my right for a change. I leaned over to kiss him on the cheek, turned the key, and drove the damn thing all the way home.

CHAPTER FOURTEEN

ON MY FIRST DAY BACK AT WORK, the previous day's interview was still echoing in my head, and I wondered if I should have mentioned my mother, or Bill. Then I wondered if I could ever see the footage myself.

When I got to the office, I was greeted at the door by Nick, who gave me a pat on the shoulder. "Grace, it's so good to see you. How are you doing?"

"I'm alright," I replied, and it was the truth.

"We saw you in the news yesterday, Grace. Please, come have a seat. There's something you need to hear."

I walked in front of him and made my way to my desk. Sitting on top it was my mug ready with coffee.

"Nick, you didn't have to—"

"I didn't. Henry made it."

I looked over at his office door and heard mumbling coming from it. I smiled at the thought of him preparing my coffee, and it was even made just as I like it.

"Please, sit down," Nick advised, and I obliged.

"Grace, we have been getting calls all morning from local news outlets."

I choked on my coffee. "W-what?"

"*Channel 3, The Philly Column,* and *Wake up, Philadelphia!* to name a few. They want to hear more."

"I . . . I can't believe it."

"Well, believe it, Grace! And *please*, take a look at the note I left. It's all the numbers of the outlets and stations. If you could at least tell them to *stop calling*, well . . ." His words trailed off, and I heard a bang in Henry's office. He had slammed the phone down, before it began ringing again.

"It would put Henry at ease," I said, finishing his sentence.

He shrugged and threw his hands up in the air. I felt like I was back in that unfamiliar dimension, like at the gathering Emilia organized. What the *hell* did they all want from me? Didn't I say enough?

I shook my head and noticed a pile of queries to my left, but I turned my attention to Nick's note first. It was a list of names and numbers, but one name stuck out to me.

Columbia County Seat – Bloomsburg.

"Nick?"

"Yes?"

"What did the county want from me?"

"Oh, right. It was a gentleman named Jonah. Yeah, he just said that he wanted to speak with you, asked for your contact information. I thought it would be best if you dealt with it," he said.

I uncapped my pen and wrote the name *Jonah* next to the number and folded the paper away into my bag. Then, I looked upon the large stack of queries to my left, begging me to read through them, took a big swig of my coffee, and got to work.

When I arrived home that evening, I went straight to the phone. It was about five-thirty, and I hoped that it wasn't too late to get an answer. I dialed the number, got it wrong the first time, and then dialed again. After a series of disheartening rings, I heard a woman's voice.

"Bloomsburg Township, how may I help you?"

"Uh, hello, my name is Grace. I received a call from this number via Stark Publishing Company."

"Oh, yes. One moment please."

I heard a beep and waited rather impatiently. Then, the line clicked as it was picked up again.

"This is Mayor Jonah Ainsworth."

The *mayor* of Bloomsburg? What the hell did he want with me? I inhaled sharply. "Yes, hi. My name is Grace, I received your message at Stark Publishing Company earlier today."

"Ah, yes, Grace. Glad you could return my call, although I am just about to exit for the day."

"I'm sorry, sir, I should have called earlier."

"No bother. Like I said, I'm glad you called. I saw your appearance on Channel 7 yesterday, and I've also read your article in *The Philadelphian*."

"You did?"

"Yes, I did indeed. I wanted to speak to you about your hometown, Centralia, that little eyesore of a town," he said unashamedly. "I'm in Bloomsburg. Do you know where that is?"

"Yes, I do. It's just north of Centralia," I responded.

"Precisely. Well, I have to say, Grace, your sudden emergence has certainly shaken the state of Pennsylvania this month. All with my support, of course . . ."

"Right," I said, unsure of what he meant.

"Listen, Grace, I'm a lot like you. I am all in favor of Centralia's permanent evacuation. Since your television appearance, your impact has reached multiple Pennsylvania cities."

"Has it?"

"It has. Centralia has personally irked me for almost two decades now, and because of your exposure, word of it has finally reached the ears and eyes of the Pennsylvania government."

"The government?"

"People talk, Grace. Word gets around quickly when you make

the news, yes?"

"Yes."

"Well, if you didn't know already, Bloomsburg holds the Columbia County seat. Grace, I'd like to set up a meeting with you, with your hometown, and with the Bloomsburg Township to discuss the future of Centralia. You've made yourself a platform now, and I want you to stand on it."

"My . . . platform?"

"Yes. We would like to hold a town meeting with the officials of Columbia County. A vote, in fact. There are a few dates that we can choose from, but I'd like to meet with you personally first to discuss this in greater detail. When are you available?"

I was flustered and dying to know what these details entailed. I pulled a pen out of my bag and set a date for an in-person meeting in Bloomsburg, Pennsylvania, in a week's time. We gave each other our regards and ended our brief call.

I nearly gave Joseph a heart attack when I walked in on him in our bedroom, combing his wavy hair .

"Joseph!"

"Jesus!" he shouted. "Welcome home, you sneak."

"I have a favor to ask you."

"Shoot."

"I need a ride, to Bloomsburg, in a week. It's in Columbia County. I'm meeting with the mayor."

He looked at me, perplexed, and set his comb down.

"In *Bloomsburg* . . . with the *mayor*? Grace, what the hell?"

"The mayor contacted *me*, Joe. Me! He wants to have Centralia evacuated, permanently. The whole town wants it, and the Pennsylvania government. A vote!"

He was starting to make sense of my jumbled words.

"Ok. Let me get this straight."

"No, wait, wait, *wait*. Let me." I took a breath and organized my thoughts. We sat on the bed together, face to face.

"Apparently my story sort of 'broke out' this month, across Pennsylvania. I've captured the attention of a lot of people, I think, and Bloomsburg holds the county seat, and . . ."

"And they want you to represent them?"

"I think so."

"To evacuate Centralia?"

I nodded.

He sighed and took my hand in his. Then he nodded, too. "Ok. Bloomsburg. A week from today."

I smiled and leaned in for a kiss.

"But, I'm coming in with you this time. You don't know these people, this person. Who did you say it is anyway?"

I pulled out the slip of paper I had and handed it to him. He examined it thoroughly and rose to his feet. "Why don't I run this by my father first?"

I nodded in agreement, because honestly, I really hadn't a clue as to what I was doing, and Richard was a very well-connected man whom I could sincerely trust.

"And, Grace, maybe you should think about getting ready for tomorrow? Bill will be arriving in the morning, right?"

"Right, good idea."

Joseph really did always know just what to say, and he was right about it, too. I removed my bag off my shoulder and placed it on my writing desk beside the photo album. My eyes lingered on it for a second, begging me to flip it open. But I knew better and pushed it aside. Instead, I turned toward our shared wardrobe. I pulled open its doors and began shuffling through my clothes. I was look-ing for one particular outfit: a blue and white gingham dress that my mother had passed down to me when I was tall enough to look like a lady in it, rather than a little girl in a potato sack. It was one of her favorites, and I thought it would be a nice thing to wear for Bill's arrival. He always said it suited me better, and she would playfully pinch at his arm when he did. It was very similar to the dress that Dorothy wore in the illustrations for *The Wizard of Oz*, one of my favorite books that Bill had given to me when I was young. I stood there, flicking through my garments, rooted in that happy memory as I got ready for the promise of tomorrow.

CHAPTER FIFTEEN

I SET MY ALARM for eight o'clock in the morning. I hopped right in the shower, then brushed my teeth, slipped on the blue and white dress, brushed my hair and headed downstairs to prepare a pot of coffee.

Bill was due to arrive around eleven-thirty, if he woke up at nine and left Centralia at nine-thirty. I wanted everything to be perfect for him; hot coffee, fresh cherry pie, and my appearance as a happy girl. All of this was for my father, who deserved a happy, heartfelt welcome while he sorted things out by my side.

Then I started on the pie. I whipped around the kitchen, flattening dough and halving fresh cherries, mixing in sugar and pinching the pastry. I heated the cherries in a saucepan until they were deliciously gooey, and I cobbled up the dough from scratch. I wanted it to be the best cherry pie he had ever eaten, homemade from the cherry-red halls of my heart. I stole one cherry for myself, and then stuck the pie dish in the oven.

I could hear the air chopping from his old car, and just in time. It was Bill in his old car, pulling up the driveway. The pie was scored and cooling on the kitchen counter. My hands were clean and, miraculously, so was my dress. I could almost hear my mother's voice around the corner, scolding me for forgetting my apron, but I was careful this time, and remembered to tie it around my waist before I even opened a cabinet. I think I had a bit of luck on my side, too. I already felt like it was going to be a lucky day.

Joseph, Emilia, and Richard positioned themselves at the foot of the stairs in the foyer, ready to greet Bill. I removed my apron, set it on the kitchen counter, and joined them. I took the lead, drew back the French doors, and slowly stepped outside to greet him.

Bill got out of the vehicle with a bag in his hand. He looked pale, tired, disheveled, and dispirited. But when he met my gaze, I saw a smile spread across his face. I ran toward him, and he dropped his bag to the ground. I closed the space between us with a leap and threw myself into his arms. He embraced me, and I squeezed him hard. Our eyes were closed, in a world of our own as we held each other close, and our heartbeats synchronized. My arms grew tired, but my heart grew fonder, and I refused to let him go.

"Dad."

"Hi Grace," he sniffled.

I pulled away at the sound and watched a single tear fall from his face before he brushed it away.

"Welcome home," I said.

He looked around him, at the sky, at the ground, at the house, then at me. "*Home*," he repeated.

Home indeed. I walked side by side with Bill, hand in hand, and we approached the door. Emilia stepped toward Bill and pulled him in for a hug, too, while Joseph and Richard tended to his bags in the car.

"Hello, Bill, do come in," Emilia begged.

We entered the house together, and I watched as the warm kitchen air swirled its way to the foyer around Bill. He took a deep inhale through his nostrils.

"Is . . . is that?"

"Wait here."

I briefly disappeared to the kitchen to grab the pie with two oven mitts for hands and returned to present it to Bill. "It's our favorite. Here—"

I held the pie under his face, and his eyes lit up like the chandelier above him, sparkling with prisms, enchanted by the golden-brown crust.

"Come, Grace. Let's prepare the pie in the dining room," Emilia said.

She escorted me forward while Richard, Joseph, and Bill stayed behind for a moment. I could hear them discussing the work arrangement, and I turned back to see Bill thanking him for his help. Richard, usually so quiet and reserved, placed both his hands on Bill's shoulders and patted them, cocking his head to maintain Bill's eye contact. I'm happy I got to see their exchange. Joseph carried his bags to the side of the stairs and offered some words of encouragement as well, and I made my way to the dinner table.

Emilia had set up five plates, with five glasses next to a pitcher of fresh milk. I placed the pie on a decadent serving tray, with a knife and server to match, and began slicing away. The men chatted away in the foyer, taking their time as I pulled a chair out for Bill and poured him a glass of milk.

"And you see the pay is very competitive here, compared to such a small town," Richard was saying.

"And the hours are better," Joseph added.

"And you will be less than twenty minutes away from this table," Emilia chimed in. She waved her hand for Bill to take his seat.

"And you'll always be welcome here, Dad," I added respectfully.

I sat beside him and lifted the first slice onto his plate while we all found our seat. Five slices later, and an empty pitcher of milk, we were comfy in each other's company. Bill noticed my dress, and jokingly referred to me as Dorothy for the remainder of the pie.

Bill agreed to stay the night with us until he was sure of himself in the city and knew where his apartment was, the location of the nearest grocery store, where to purchase milk as fresh as that from the pitcher, and where he would be starting work. He would be making the transition from ash and coal to cement, glass, and granite. Richard planned to introduce Bill to his new boss, as well as establish a connection with the local mechanic to fix up that "unsightly machine" of his, as he called the car. Bill was just as lucky as I was, as well as unlucky as me. He never had to return to Centralia, and that was the solid truth now, solid like the ground below him.

After our pie, Joseph slipped me the photo album behind my back. "Why don't you head out to the garden? I'm sure you could use the fresh air."

I grabbed the album and led Bill toward the daylight through the glass doors. It was just the two of us.

I took a seat at the small garden table, and Bill joined me with another glass of milk.

"How are you doing, Dad?"

"I'm . . . better. Now that I'm with you, kiddo." He gulped down the whole glass of milk as if to justify his words. I just watched and smiled.

"Dad . . . I wanted to apologize. I should have been there for you. I should have—"

"Grace, please. You've already done so much more than you had to. For me and for your mother."

I looked down at the album in my lap.

"Don't worry about me, Grace. I'm *here*. I'm out . . . and . . . your mother is, too."

I swallowed that lump in my throat and reached across the table to hold his hand.

"It's so good to see your face," I said, and he smiled back at me.

"It's so good to see my Grace."

I slid the album across the table toward him.

"What's this?" he asked.

"Open it."

He turned the cover to reveal the first page, and his face opened up like a book. He flipped through each page, smiling, and tilting his head. He stopped on the photo of my mother and me sitting at the café.

"Remember the cafe menus?" I asked.

"We were in way over our heads!" he chuckled.

Bill released a sigh as he flipped to the photo of the two of them standing beside each other, my mother looking to the ground, smiling bashfully, while he watched her with the light of love in his eyes.

"She was so happy that day. I'd never seen her glow like that. It was all because of you, Grace. I hope you know that."

We reminisced together in the midday sun, bending and crinkling the album's pages, hopeful for better days to come for the both of us. I told him to keep the photo album, and he accepted it with adoration.

Later, Bill was set up in the living room for the night, and he was already looking livelier than when he arrived. I sat by him at the edge of the couch while he dozed off. I could see the color return to his face as if the cherry pie really was baked with love.

I decided that I didn't want to tell him about Bloomsburg. He had only just arrived and settled in, and I didn't want to bring up the town again. He needed to heal, to move forward, and he deserved that peace. I couldn't save my birth father, or Sam, or my mother. But I had Bill, here and now, right in front of me, and I would never, ever let him out of my sight again.

I tiptoed my way across the living area, up the stairs to the bedroom and joined Joseph in bed.

"Hey you."

"Hey, Joe, what do you know?"

I settled down onto his chest and listened to his heartbeat as it rose and fell with his breaths, fluid and relaxed.

"Everything feels like it's falling into place." I spoke in a hushed tone.

He pulled my chin up to face him and pushed the hair away from my eyes. "It's not falling, Grace. You're putting the pieces together."

I thought of Sam and his Eiffel Tower model, and how it felt when I placed the topper on with him. Joseph pulled me in for a kiss, and I kissed him back, long and with longing. Everyone I loved was in the same place again, and all I could do was feel it all. To love and be loved, was all that mattered to me in that moment.

CHAPTER SIXTEEN

BILL WAS ALWAYS ABLE TO take what life threw at him, and not just because of the trauma he had to endure. Before the accident, he was still a hardworking, fearless coal miner in the eyes of my father. Bill was the son of a single mother growing up without a father of his own, and he took care of his mother the way he did mine before she passed away. He had been built for a life of deconstruction and reconstruction. It was only fitting that he'd get back to work with his burly hands and strong mind to help to build and develop America's Next Great City.

Bill and I arrived at his new apartment in Alleghany West, just the two of us. Richard handed us the key, and we hopped straight into his "unsightly machine" to revel in the next milestone together. The apartment was a large studio with hardwood flooring, a washer and dryer, and all working light bulbs. There was not much inside, but it was furnished with a bed, couch, floor lamp, and a bookcase. A day of unpacking, some opened windows, and a few books to line the bookshelf would soon liven the place up.

We climbed the stairs to the third floor together with all of his bags in multiple trips, without forgetting to pay the meter for street parking. Joseph offered his strength for the job, but I knew that I could handle it. After everything was unloaded, we fell onto the couch together, to be greeted by a puff of dust. It was close quarters; nothing quite like Richard and Emilia's cottage-style mini-mansion, but it was a nice place indeed.

"Whew," I sighed.

"Thanks for the help, kiddo."

"So, what do you think?"

Bill looked around the room, taking in all four white walls that he could call home now.

"It's a lot better with you here," he stated.

"I'll come see you," I promised, "whenever you want, Dad."

He was fixated on one of his suitcases, and I became stuck on it, too. He got up, crouched down beside it, and unzipped it. From the suitcase, he slowly lifted a silver urn. I quickly rose to my feet, and he held it toward me, like a newborn child.

"Is that—?"

He nodded.

Cradling the precious urn in one arm, I turned toward the bookcase, examining it intently. Then I blew strongly at its middle shelf and whisked away dust with my spare hand, clearing a final resting place for my dear mother. Together, we carefully positioned her in the center and slowly stood back.

"She's at peace now, Dad. Just as she wanted."

He looked down to the floor and nodded. "Maybe now I can be, too," he proclaimed.

I helped him to unpack the rest of his bags and boxes, full of clothes, bedding, toiletries, kitchen plates and utensils; all the things that made up my old home. In a way, I was happy that they had made it out of Centralia, too.

One box looked much older than the others, and much smaller. I flipped it around to face me and saw *Sam* written on the side. My eyes lingered on it for just a moment before I pulled back the top. Sam's Lincoln Logs, the Eiffel Tower model, his flashlight, colored pencils, and some of his architectural designs sat neatly on top of each other, lined at the bottom by some of his old clothes, and an old candle with a box of matches.

I removed the candle and brought it over to the bookshelf, placing it to the right of my mother's ashes. Bill took notice, and an idea appeared on his face. He moved away and dipped into a separate box, retrieving the photo album, and set it to the left of her.

I squeezed the matchbox in my hand. "Dad, I know you don't want a funeral, but how about we say a few words?"

Bill closed his eyes and nodded. "Ok, kiddo."

I struck a match and gingerly passed its flame onto the wick, and blew out the match. Bill reached down to hold my hand in his and began to speak. "I don't know what to say," he admitted.

"Sure you do," I encouraged.

He looked up to the ceiling for a moment and then closed his eyes. "Rita ... my dear." The apartment grew silent as the day began to fade away. "We know that you struggled ... and ... and we just wanted to take your pain away ..."

I held my breath and held back a tear.

"I know you're at peace now, and I know you're with Sam and ... and ... and I love you, my dear. I love you, and I'm sorry it had to be this way."

He was squeezing my hand hard, and I brushed my thumb over top of his, shaking it slightly to comfort him. He swayed in his gait and took a deep breath. "*Haah,*" he sighed, turning toward me.

I started to think about the last time I spoke with my mother. It was the morning after our day trip in the city. She and Bill were ready to take the drive back to Centralia, exhausted by the bright and busy world that Philadelphia boasted. They'd said their goodbyes to Joseph, Richard, and Emilia. Bill climbed into the car, and I held my mother's arm as she dipped into the car seat. Before shutting the door, she pulled me in for one last embrace. It was long, and she held tight, almost as if she knew it would be our last. I had my eyes closed the entire time, focusing only on the feel of her. She whispered into my ear.

"Thank you, Grace. Thank you."

It was the last thing she had said to me.

"Of course. I love you, mother."

She kissed me hard on the cheek before releasing our embrace. "I'll see you soon," I added. Those were my last words to her, and I believed that they would be true.

I now felt my stomach begin to knot up. I took a deep breath and exhaled, causing the candlelight to flicker and reflect across the urn like a spark jumping away from a fire. "I love you, mother. Rest now, and please . . ."

I squeezed Bill's hand. "Take care of Sam."

CHAPTER SEVENTEEN

JOSEPH AND I BOTH woke at seven o'clock. We mirrored each other's morning routines and breakfast. I drank my cup o' joe with Joe, although I did require a stronger one compared to his. It had been like that since the interview, and I was leaning more toward a black cup of it these days. Black coffee is simple, straightforward, and bold, and that's how I wanted the meeting to go that day.

Bloomsburg is about a half hour north of Centralia, just over a two-hour drive from Northeast Philadelphia, and it is worth the wait. We made it past the city line and pulled up to the mayor's office, avoiding Centralia along the way, and therefore sparing Joseph from its cursed air.

Bloomsburg is a quaint yet busy little place. Its streets are lined with small businesses, red brick townhomes, and it even has its own university. I immediately saw why it holds the county seat. The mayor's office was inside the belly of Bloomsburg Town Hall—a tall, beige structure off Main Street with a large American Flag waving high in the air at the front.

"Grace, are you *sure* you don't want me to come in?" Joseph asked.

"I'm sure," I said confidently and against his wishes.

"Alright, but you owe me one," he joked in return.

We parked the car in front of the building, and I placed my feet on the new ground. When I walked inside, I could finally put a face to the woman who fielded my phone call the week before. She was sipping on a cup of coffee that looked black as coal, and it gave me a boost of confidence.

"Are you Jonah's ten o'clock?" she inquired.

"Yes. My name is Grace."

She didn't say anything. Instead, she set her coffee down, got up, and walked over to the door closest to her, heels clicking and echoing loudly around her, and then gave three little knocks.

"Sir, your ten o'clock has arrived," she said through the door.

A few seconds passed before it was opened by a plump, pleasant looking man with silver hair and a bright red bow tie: Mr. Jonah Ainsworth, Mayor of Bloomsburg.

"Grace, so nice to meet you."

He approached me with a sudden handshake and brought along a waft of air with him. It carried the scent of strong coffee, which put me at ease as I imagined that we were both on the same tier of caffeination.

"Please, please, come in. Have a seat."

I followed him into the small office, and he closed the door behind me. In the corner, I noticed that he used the same coffee maker that I used at work, glowing with that familiar red-orange switch light.

"Did you find it here ok?"

"I did, thanks."

"Excellent. Now, let's get right to it, shall we?"

He clasped his hands together and rested them on the desk that separated us. On it there was an aloe plant, a small white lamp, translucent pendulum balls clacking away at each other, and the source of the smell—a steaming coffee mug.

"I was so moved by your story, Grace. Truly," he started. "And to be perfectly honest, I agree with every facet of it, as does most of Pennsylvania, now."

I smiled. "That's such a relief to hear."

"I'm sure. Centralia has been on my radar ever since the day it erupted. Did you know that we could see it from here? The smoke?"

I shook my head.

"For a week we watched the plume grow larger and heavier and turn into a storm cloud over the town, not to mention the awful smell."

Ah yes, that familiar smell again.

"This all happened before my position as mayor, of course. But even then, it was always insignificant to us." He took a sip of his piping hot coffee and sucked in the air through his teeth to cool off his mouth. "You don't know how many complaints we've received over the years."

He pointed to a file cabinet behind him that was just about ready to burst with papers. I imagined it being the first thing to burn up if this city had caught fire, too.

"There are folks like you, who can't believe it's in any way lawful to have a community on top of such dangerous land."

I nodded in agreement.

"There are also people who just can't stand the look of it or the smell of it."

I visualized the papers in the cabinet going up in flames, and the metal drawers beginning to warp and melt away.

"Then there are the Centralians, and there are fifty of them remaining. Fifty. Almost all who stay in Centralia by *choice*. Do you know why, Grace?"

I thought of my mother as a statistic: number *fifty-one*. I turned my attention to his eyes.

"Yes. Yes, I do."

"Why's that?" he asked.

"Because Centralia is their home, and you *can't* make them leave it."

"But maybe we *can*," he insisted.

He had my attention now, and the flames all over the file cabinet vanished.

"When it happened, I tried to get in touch with *your* mayor; unfortunately, he was caught in the rubble of his own home when the blast occurred. Did you know that?"

I pictured the mayor as a man in a black suit and tie walking down to his basement after hearing a rumble, and then I pictured the ground giving way beneath him into a pit of despair.

"No," I replied.

"There *is* no mayor of Centralia. There is no one, not *one* person governing your town. It's almost as if the state of Pennsylvania completely ignores Centralia, just sweeping it all under the rug, just as they did with the damned zip code, right?"

"It certainly feels that way," I returned.

"So, then. I conducted a little research; if a town chooses to become de facto independent, to be governed by the townsfolk themselves, then there has to be a meeting with the county seat for approval, or denial."

I imagined fifty people standing in the middle of the road I grew up on, glaring at me with daggers for eyes.

"And we've done it. We've got a date set for it and everything. All because of you, Grace."

"What do you mean?"

"You shook Pennsylvania this month, with your article and your interview. You've opened up many pairs of eyes, and unclogged equal pairs of ears."

I chewed my lip and watched the pendulum balls swing back and forth.

"On October 14, in this very building, the halls will be flooded with Centralians, maybe all, maybe few, to claim their right as an independent township . . . and Grace, I would like you to oppose them, maybe say a few words and attend the meeting in favor of Bloomsburg."

"Oppose them? And represent you?"

He spun in his chair and pulled a file out of his file cabinet, now aflame again, and opened it up.

"Represent *us*," he corrected. "Here, I've written a proposal on evacuating the last fifty residents. We, the town of Bloomsburg, will give a three-week grace period for said residents to sort out their affairs, as well as providing a lowered rate to our financial assistance programs, to help get them back on their feet."

He laid out the file in front of me, and I scanned it.

"Also, with the clear evidence that the fire still burns underground today, I've consulted with the county to outsource and contract laborers and have the town filled in with dirt. Gone."

He pinched the pendulum balls together and ended the clacking.

"Of course, they are going to rebel. They're going to defy it and say whatever they can to convince the Columbia County officials that they are thriving, despite our extensive record of death certificates and missing persons cases within the perimeter of the town."

"And despite all that's happened to me," I gulped.

"*Exactly.*"

I sighed.

"But listen, Grace. We have a soapbox now, and you do, too. You're the *only* person who made it out alive who's actually said something about it. You spoke up, and now you can actually *do* something about it."

I met his eyes and nodded with a smile.

"We're on your side, Grace. A hell of a lot of us are. It's up to you if you want to be a part of this. We're not out of the woods yet, but we have our chance."

Out of the woods, just as the buck had wanted to be when he approached the town, I thought.

I picked up the documents and reviewed them. It was all there in front of me, just as he said. There were contracts, letters, invoices, and designs on where the filling in would take place. It was straightforward and bold, but not so simple.

Jonah had been requesting a mine inspection with the U.S. Bureau of Mines for years, and it was all in the writing. First and foremost, the sound of the accident had quite literally moved him, and the tiny bit of press that covered it had prompted him to take action. He had grown a soft spot for the town, and I could hear it in his voice. If only he could have been my mayor.

The fact that there were still people living on top of the mine was enough for the bureau to keep dismissing his letters—that and the fact that the entrance had caved in on top of those twelve miners, my father included, meant that there would be no way for them to inspect it anyway. At the back of the file were some photographs of Centralia depicting abandoned buildings, holes in the ground, smoke and ash everywhere, and, in the very last photograph, the scorched body of a dead dog on the side of the road. I felt a wave of heat flow over me, and I quickly slapped the file shut.

I placed the documents down and tried to take control of my breathing. *Not now,* I thought. *Just breathe.*

"Mayor Ainsworth," I said, "I'd be more than happy to attend this town meeting."

He narrowed his eyes and displayed a rewarding smile.

"I thought that you might." He slid the file back toward him and shoved it back into the filing cabinet.

"What do you know about mine reclamation, Grace?"

"Not as much as you, I'm sure."

"The thing is, with all of these reports on missing townsfolk, and now your story being broadcast, it should be obvious that a mine inspection isn't necessary."

"I couldn't agree more," I added.

"And if the town is as strong and sturdy as these Centralians claim it to be, then what harm would it be for them to send some-body out there for a *ground* inspection?"

"A ground inspection? But I'm not sure that's what they're paid to do, Mr. Ainsworth."

"Oh, they aren't. It's not about the money. I guarantee that if they sent one person, just one person to your sinkhole-scattered town, they would agree with me."

"Agree with what?"

"Like I said, I did a little research. I believe that the mines can be filled in without any digging needed to be done at all."

It took me a moment to fully understand what he was saying, then I thought of Sam.

"The holes."

"Yes, Grace. Every last one of them."

He took the last sip of his coffee and wiped a bead of sweat off his forehead.

"There is a process called hydraulic flushing. Rock deposits, dirt, and water are injected straight down onto the fire, dousing it in slurry that would dry over into a crust."

"So . . . so they wouldn't go down there, would they?"

"They wouldn't have to, and to be honest, I think that's what they're *afraid* of."

"I can't blame them," I said.

"They try to shrug it off as some regulation, throwing away every attempt I've made to try to make them see things my way. They're just cowards, shaking like leaves at the thought of going near the town."

"I just can't believe it. The U.S. Bureau of Mines has known about this for a long time."

"*Years*, Grace. Too many of them."

My forehead was getting hot, too, and I could feel the sweat starting to appear.

"All this time, Grace. You've been there all this time, you and God knows how many other children . . . standing on the ground you lived on for your entire youth. It sickens me."

It sickened me, too. My town wasn't just some dark place that was cut off from the rest of the world; it was purposefully ignored and denied any help.

"I just can't believe this. How could they get away with this?"

"I hate to say it, Grace, but small-town folk just don't get the attention they deserve anymore."

I nodded.

"But you've gained the attention that we needed, Grace."

I thought for a moment about the bureau and its workers. I was furious at them for treating my town like it was a lost cause. It really was swept under the rug by ignorant or fearful men, or both. Then I thought about the gaps in the road. They were scary, even for me. I could see why an outsider would want to avoid working in the town, and I hated to admit it, but I sympathized with them.

"It would be dangerous work for them, wouldn't it? I understand why they're afraid."

"Sure it would, but so is walking to the bus stop, like you said in your article."

Perspiration now trailed down my temple.

"The way I see it, Grace, is that there isn't any other choice. Dozens of people have died or gone missing in the past two decades, and I'm sure that these workers know what they're doing. They'd have to tread carefully around the roads, of course. But if they aren't the ones to do it, just to fill it in one time, then it will be another generation of misfortunate children tiptoeing their way through a short life."

I wiped away the sweat and readjusted myself in the chair. He was right. It all felt right, but still, I didn't want anyone else to die by Centralia.

"Still with me, Grace?"

"Yes, Mr. Ainsworth. I just—I want this to be the end of it."

"As do I, Miss Grace. As do I."

"I will be there, Mr. Ainsworth. You can count on that."

"Excellent. I look forward to seeing you. Mark your calendar, Grace. This isn't a date to forget."

"Believe me, Mr. Ainsworth, I couldn't forget if I tried."

Joseph waited outside the hall for me. As I exited the building, I tried my best to appear confident. I climbed into the car seat beside him.

"How was it, Grace?"

"There's going to be a town meeting here, with the county, the U.S. Bureau of Mines, and some of my old neighbors, probably."

"Bureau of Mines? That's a thing?"

"I didn't know either," I replied.

"Joseph, they *knew* about the accident. They knew from the start and didn't do anything about it."

"You can't be serious."

"Dead serious. Mayor Ainsworth had been reaching out to them for years, and . . . well, my story has made it all such a public issue that something might actually be done about it."

"You mean, filling in the mine."

"Yes. The entrance caved in on the day of the blast, so they never did an inspection, out of fear or just not giving a shit about it."

Joseph leaned closer to me and took my hand in his as I grew hot with frustration.

"There is a way, though," I continued. "To fill it in without going down there."

"How's that?"

"The holes, like the one Sam fell through. They could fill them."

Joseph squeezed my hand tightly. "How do you feel about this, Grace?"

I looked up to the sky for a moment. "He would be buried there. Sam, he'd be there forever." I looked over to Joseph and squeezed his hand back. "But maybe it's not such a bad thing."

"Maybe not," he added.

"If it does get filled in, the men who would do it could . . . they could die, Joseph."

Joseph leaned back onto the headrest and sighed.

"And then it would be an accident. All over again," I said.

Joseph whipped his head toward me and leaned in further. "You can't think like that, Grace. It's not . . . it's not your problem anymore."

"You're wrong. It's always my problem, Joseph. What if another twelve workers die? Another father or son lost to Centralia?"

"Grace, listen." Joseph took my head into his hands. "This is the best thing for the town, I really think so. You have to weigh the good against the bad. *Nobody* has to die. *Nobody* else."

I blinked away at his gaze, but he pulled me right back into it.

"Believe in yourself, Grace. You've come this far; so much has happened. Don't think of it as another loss—that's not what this is. It's an opportunity. Remember that, Grace."

I closed my eyes and leaned my head on his hand.

"Grace, I believe in you," he stated.

I inhaled through my nose and nodded. He ran one hand through my hair and the other across my cheek.

"It's gonna be ok, Grace."

"I hope so," I added.

Joseph pulled his hands away and put them on the wheel. "Ready to go home?"

"Ready."

He leaned in close for a kiss on my forehead, turned the key, and drove us home.

CHAPTER EIGHTEEN

IN THE DAYS THAT FOLLOWED, it felt like I had entered a state of metamorphosis. At work, I was blowing through the pile of queries on my desk, reading through the works of aspiring novelists and making calls to them, creating publishing proposals with Henry's approval, making coffee, and making small talk with Nick. It was nice to be caught up with work and to be back in the swing of things again.

After work, I took the bus to Alleghany West to see Bill. I badly wanted to tell him about the plans for Centralia, but nothing was certain, and I didn't want to disappoint or bring up the past. Instead, I was doing what any normal woman would do; visit family for the sake of family.

"So how is work going, Dad?"

He passed me a glass of cold milk and joined me on his sofa, sans dust. His apartment continued to look more and more like home, sweet home.

"It's . . . different. It's tough work, kiddo. But it's above ground, and it is worth it."

We both took a gulp of milk.

"Oh, and guess what? I got a little work done on the car."

"Oh, really?" I asked.

"Yeah, it's going to be a long journey for it, but it's a start."

I'd never noticed how blue Bill's eyes were until he came to

Philadelphia, and they were shining just a little brighter now. He looked better in this world, a world away from inhaling smoke and coal dust. Someone without a clue about Centralia might laugh at the thought of city air being fresh air, but it certainly was to Bill and me.

"Thank goodness," I teased, "it's about time it got a little tender loving care."

A buildup of ash and dirt on his car had been waxed away to reveal a make and model. This old beater had a name, and its name was *1954 Chevy Nova*. It was just one of those things that I would never have known thanks to Centralia. I couldn't wait to bury it all under dirt.

Bill and I chatted about city life, his aching hands, a funny query I'd received about an erotic memoir, and he revealed that he'd started reading Nick's mystery novel that I had lent him. I'd never really had a moment like this with Bill before. I wanted to live inside of it, or to preserve it in a book so that I may flip to its page whenever I wanted and read over it, forever bookmarked by a piece of my heart.

Each morning I eagerly arrived at work, greeted by my friend and colleague, Nick. Each evening, I went home to Joseph, and we swapped who made dinner on rotating days. Some days I visited Bill, and some days he visited us. There was always enough cherry pie to go around, as well as daily anecdotes and discussions on current events. I think I felt happier, and I looked forward to the future again.

On the night before the Bloomsburg vote, Joseph lay in bed next to me, face to face. "Are you ready for tomorrow?" he asked.

It was a big question that required a lot of breath, and a lot of thought.

"I've . . . been waiting for this day my entire life."

Joseph smiled that sweet smile of his. "You say that a lot now."

Joseph would be the dictionary definition of a good lover. He is considerate, understanding, and supportive of me, and has been from the start.

"Why do you put up with it all?" I asked.

"With what?" Joseph returned.

"I mean, all of it, all of *me*. The . . . the baggage I carry."

He huffed out a breath and placed two fingers around the little book-shaped locket I wore around my neck since the day he gave it to me. He snapped open its silver page where it read *Love You Always*. He brought his dark eyes back up to mine. "I just thought you could use some help carrying that baggage, and you look a lot happier because of it."

He always knows what to say.

The next day was going to be big, when the meeting of two powerful forces would reach temperatures hot enough to burn cities. But that night, I was lucky. My anxieties, fears, hopes and dreams were equally silent in my mind, allowing me to fall sound asleep as the fading light of the cool October twilight deepened to the color of black onyx.

CHAPTER NINETEEN

*October 14, 1980. Columbia County and The People of Centralia
Discuss Evacuation Plans.*

THERE WERE FLYERS ALL AROUND Bloomsburg inviting the townsfolk and their families to see the freak show. Joseph accompanied
me, and I wouldn't have wanted it any other way. We pulled up to
the Town Hall together once again, stomachs full of coffee and
nerves, hearts full of love, and minds full of reason.

The parking lot was full, but luckily the side streets were a little
more forgiving. Joseph wore that gray suit and red tie again, while
I wore one of my mother's old dresses that Bill had unpacked: a
black, knee length, A-line dress with a pair of modest black ballet
flats. I could feel her in that dress, hugging my body the way that
she embraced me last.

After parking the car, Joseph rushed over to grab the door for
me, and walked with me hand in hand to the gates of the township. I did not hesitate when I took my first step in. Inside, I was
led to the council hall by the receptionist and was then faced with
a mess of people, but it was clear to me who was who. The people
of Bloomsburg were a burst of color and chatter to the left; to the
right were the twelve people who had unearthed themselves from
Centralia to be here today. They sat with gray faces, stringy hair,
tattered clothing, and an overall look of bitterness about them.

Only I could see the smoke that hovered above their heads.

The room was divided, and all the while watched by a line of men and women, sitting along a long table, dressed for business: Columbia County officials, Mayor Jonah Ainsworth, Bloomsburg Town Council members, a member of the Bureau of Mines, and one mandatory member of the State Senate. There was a seat reserved for me at the front of the Bloomsburg side of the room. As if to close the room, I took my seat and gave a nod to the mayor. The chatter around me lessened to a murmur as people shot looks my way. Then, he began.

"Good morning, everyone, from near or far. My name is Jonah Ainsworth, Mayor of Bloomsburg, seat of Columbia County."

One by one, the people sitting at the council table all stood as they introduced themselves to a crowd of both anxious and interested characters. I couldn't pay them any mind, though. I was distracted. I turned to my right and examined the Centralians. I didn't recognize any of them, and I was grateful for it.

"We've gathered this meeting today with the people of Centralia, the township of Bloomsburg, the U.S. Bureau of Mines, and the Pennsylvania State Government to come to a conclusion by vote of either the permanent evacuation and landfill of the town of Centralia, or the grant of Independent Township to the town of Centralia."

Mayor Jonah went over a series of rules, much like the ones I was given by Kelly O'Connor at Studio 7 News, but much more broken down: be civil, be opportunistic, and listen intently.

It started with Bloomsburg, and the mayor went over the proposal once more, exactly as he had with me, word for word even, as if he had been waiting for this day for his whole life, too.

Evacuation, deconstruction, filling in, road blockage.

I could see the State Senator looking satisfied with the devised plan as he jotted down some scribbles on legal paper. Jonah was then addressed with a series of grunts and low chatter by Centralia. After some stirring, it was Centralia's turn to take the floor.

A middle-aged, pale-faced man in an old, loosely fitted black shirt, dark blue overalls, and black hobnail boots stood slowly. His brow was deeply furrowed into the center of his wrinkled face. He directed his voice to the mayor and said, "It were not best that we should all think alike; it is difference in opinion that makes horse races."

His voice hit me like a plume of hot smoke. This man, this sick, sad-looking man, was quoting Mark Twain. I could not believe what he had said. He looked over at me for a split second before turning back to the mayor.

That was *my* persuasion tactic. To quote Mark Twain was a weapon I had used to back myself up, and I often live by Twain's words of wisdom. So how could somebody so horribly stuck on the wrong end of justice quote the same man as me? This man was my enemy. He was my foe, my adversary. He spoke bitterly. Nevertheless, at one time he was also my neighbor.

Another man stood up, hand in hand with someone I assumed was his wife, and threw in his piece as well. "Almost thirty years we've been living in Centralia, and not once were we affected by the incident."

His wife added, "We've lived off the land for generations, all of us in Centralia have. We're an adaptable folk. We can and we *will* live off the land for generations to come, and a hole in the road is not going to put a stop to our daily life."

I was squeezing my hands so hard that my knuckles cracked. I turned around to look at Joseph standing in the back of the hall, who shared the same disgruntled look that I wore.

The woman continued, "My husband works in the mines and finds coal every day. The town sits on top of a mountain of it. To get rid of my town is to waste our only resource!"

The other Centralians hooted and hollered amongst each other while Bloomsburg mumbled in disagreement. The woman's husband spoke again: "It's true. I see it every day. There are a few veins of tunnels below us that we mine, and they're cut off from the mine fire. I go below every day, I walk up on it every day, and let me tell you that anything that is damned enough to fall through a crack in the ground was damned by God himself, not fit enough to live in a town as strong as ours."

Centralia whistled and cheered at him as he took back to his seat. I closed my fists, then closed my eyes and saw Sam being damned by God himself. When I opened my eyes, I saw red. I shot up from my chair.

"Mayor Ainsworth, I'd like to speak now," I blurted out.

He looked over to the council members, then back to me and gave me a nod, followed by an introduction.

"Yes, of course. Here we have Grace, a young woman who grew up in Centralia until she was old enough to leave on her own. You may have seen her on the news recently or read her article in the paper. Go ahead, Grace."

I heard the chattering of Bloomsburg behind me, but instead I faced Centralia. I took a deep breath and began.

"When I was sixteen, I was standing at my bus stop after school with my little brother, Sam," I said. "He was waiting for me, standing on the road, when it opened up underneath him, and swallowed him whole. I ran after him, not even looking where I was stepping. I grabbed his hand to try to save him, but he slipped."

The muttering behind me slowed down to a full stop.

"He was just ten years old, a *child*. *Ten years old*!"

I wasn't holding back anymore. I walked over to the center aisle that separated both sides of the room and stood in the middle, staring the gray man in the face, while I felt hot tears streaming down mine.

"Sam wanted to be an architect when he grew up, so that he could rebuild the town, and make it viable again—truly viable, with a hospital, safe schools, a post office, and more. He was ten years old, and he *knew* that he wasn't living a normal life. He knew it, and every day he dreamed of a world where he could make it better for *everyone*. He grew up in Centralia without ever leaving. He never had the *chance*."

I looked over to Joseph again and could feel my hands shaking. I closed them into fists and then straightened my arms to my sides.

"If nothing is accomplished in this meeting today, then the future of Centralia's children will be no different than my brother Sam's. The children, more than *anyone* else, deserve a chance at a better life."

I wiped away the tears and turned toward Bloomsburg.

"They deserve a life with *solid* ground, a life with *clean* air! They deserve a life with access to a hospital within a half mile from their home, a home that sits on a *leveled* foundation. They deserve a life with schools that would teach them about Earth Science, not how to avoid areas of a town where the earth is too fragile to support even the weight of a *thought*. A life full of blue skies that they can watch clouds float across—not clouds of smoke and ash but real clouds. And most of all, they deserve a life with a *living* family, not one where they wonder if their father will *ever* be returning from the burning tunnels below."

I looked back at the mayor and sighed.

"I wish that I could have that for myself as a child. It's all I ever wanted. It's what every child deserves, and this I know is true. So, when you cast your vote today, if you can find it in your heart, please think about my little brother, Sam, and then make a decision that you can *live* with."

I was drifting in a sea of my tears and other folks' whispers, but somehow I felt all alone. Everything was fading around me, and even the colorful Bloomsburg crowd began to turn gray. I was back home, in Centralia, standing on the gray road surrounded by gray sky. The twelve Centralians all stared at me with their dead, corrupted eyes, feet planted firmly on shaky ground. There was nothing left for me to say. So, I got up, caught Mayor Jonah's eye once more, and then walked away.

I passed by the Centralians, passed by Joseph, pushed through the hall's doors, the receptionist, and then the front doors. The sunlight blinded me when my feet hit the pavement, and I felt my path start to shift to the left. I followed it, leaned against the red brick of the building, and vomited.

Joseph ran after me and found me outside in my altered state. He gently approached me and placed two trustworthy hands on my back. He brought me back to life as I adjusted my posture, and then he walked me back to the car.

"Come on, Grace. It's over now. Let's go home."

CHAPTER TWENTY

THE RIDE BACK TO PHILADELPHIA was a blur for me, and it was swift. Joseph may have ignored the speed limits as we crossed county lines, but he had his reasons. I could sense that he was as exasperated as I was. It was his first time sharing the room with Centralia, and he was visibly thwarted by their presence back in the town hall. They had left a lingering, burnt taste in our mouths.

Joseph pulled into the driveway, put the car in park, and reached over the seat to pull my face to look at him.

"Hey."

"Hi."

"Grace, are you ok? You've been really quiet."

I could still taste the vomit in my mouth. "I think I just need to clean up."

He nodded and rubbed the back of my head before we both entered the house.

Upstairs in our bedroom, I kicked off my shoes, peeled off my dress that was stuck to my body with sweat, and ran my hands through my hair. I wrapped a towel around myself and headed to the bathroom. First, I brushed my teeth, ridding my tongue of the awful taste in my mouth, but unfortunately, it could not relieve the ashy taste that the town folk left behind. The water eventually washed it all away, pure and clear down the drain.

Then I imagined that Sam's death could have looked better

had he died by water; submerged, still and pale, floating and calm. Compared to the fire, smoldering, gray and black.

With these thoughts, I could not breathe properly. I gripped my knees as some sort of grounding technique to rid my mind of these intrusive thoughts. It did not work until I dug my nails into my kneecaps. It did hurt, but it distracted me from my mind. Many people say that distraction is a crucial way to deal with physical pain. But what if you live a life where physical pain is the only distraction from your inner pain?

I looked over to the tub, inserted the plug, and turned on the faucets to draw myself a bath. I let the water run until a layer of steam lingered just below the edge. Then I removed my towel, folded it, and hung it over the edge of the sink. I lowered myself into the water, which quickly emptied my lungs of all the air inside.

The water was burning hot. My body shuddered at the sting of it as I forced myself against the tub, and I watched my skin turn from a pink blush to a vermillion red, but I refused to emerge from it. The pain was all that I could think about, but I didn't *want* it to end. My eyes were watering from the heat, and I could feel every inch of my body scalding. I only focused on the pain, as it demanded me too, and it obliterated all the thoughts that were plaguing my mind. I winced as my skin seared and my body began to shake. The blood was rushing to the scar on my hand, causing it to flash from red to white with my racing heartbeat. I tried to hold it in for as long as I could, sitting in this scorching moment of thoughtlessness, but an audible gasp seeped out of me like I was a kettle ready to be poured. I quickly shot out of the water, ending my self-imposed misery and climbed over the edge to the safety of the cold tile. The shock of the temperature change caused me to gasp again as I writhed on the floor.

Joseph heard my struggle from the bedroom and threw the door open, revealing my naked, cherry-red body trembling on the floor.

"Grace!"

He threw a towel around me and scooped me up from the floor. It hurt to be touched, but I didn't care.

"Shhh. It's ok. It's ok," he repeated, holding me close to his chest, rocking back and forth.

I didn't want him to see me like this. I was so ashamed of myself. "I'm just as bad as the rest of them," I cried. "Look at me! I'm *just* like them!"

"You're *not*," he said sternly. "You are *nothing* like them, Grace!" Joseph held my face in his hands. "Grace, the first night I met you, you looked at me like a stranger. I was in your way, and you couldn't care less about me, what I had to say, or what I was even doing outside the dorms." Joseph leaned in closer. "But when I told you I had got locked out and was probably going to sleep out there, leaning against the door, you offered me a place to sleep anyway."

"Well, what kind of person would I be if I just walked away from you?" I asked through streaming tears.

"That's what I mean. You helped me, even when you didn't want to, because you couldn't stand to see someone being left out in the cold. That's how you're different, Grace. The rest of them, they don't care who gets left behind. But you do."

His words made sense for a moment, and I wished that I could spend every moment of my life listening to them. Even though he always said what I needed to hear, I couldn't get the words to stick this time. It was all too much. Images of the buck, of my mother, and Sam flashed through my mind, completely out of my control, while Joseph held me tighter. All I could do was feel it all, the pains in my head. I wanted to go back into the tub, to feel my flesh burn so I wouldn't have to think anymore. But he wouldn't let me go. I cried and cried and cried until I was completely empty. Then it happened to me again: I blacked out.

Much like the last time, I woke up in my bed, with Joseph

kneeling on the floor by me. He was staring at me with such apprehension. I couldn't look him in the eye. I curled my knees close to my chest and squeezed my pillow, too embarrassed to do anything.

"I'm sorry," I said.

"Don't be," he replied.

"I . . . I think there's something wrong with me," I admitted. "Sometimes I just can't think straight. Or breathe. It just . . . takes over."

Joseph nodded, and I tried not to cry again.

"I believe you, Grace. You've been through hell."

I conjured up the courage to look at him.

"Grace, we can help you. I think maybe you should talk to somebody about this."

What he said frightened me, and I was sure of what he meant.

"See? I'm *just* as crazy as them," I said.

"No, Grace. You aren't. Anybody who had lived through what you have would be just the same."

Emilia appeared at the doorway with a slip of paper clutched in her worried hands. I rose to a sitting position, and she carefully walked to the edge of the bed to sit by me. She handed me the piece of paper. On it had a name, address, and a phone number.

"Grace, dear. This is for you if you need it." She paused and glanced over at Joseph, and him to her. "She specializes in the kind of help that we think you could benefit from, dear."

Joseph placed a hand on my shoulder and sat beside me, too.

"We just want what's best for you," she finished.

I stared at the paper. It read: *Mrs. Ida Thorstein – Philadelphia, PA*

I looked at my hand, still crimson from my episode earlier, and it stung. The scar had been open for months now, and I'd just made it worse. I looked back up to Emilia, nodded my head, and agreed to go. There wasn't much left for them to say, and I wasn't one to argue with them. They were right.

I'd been feeling like I was losing control for a while now and figured I didn't have much else to lose. One thing I knew for sure is that I didn't want to end up like my mother, hurting myself to silence the noise in my head.

"Ok. I'll go," I said. "I will."

I called to set an appointment with her, and the call was very brief. I gave my name and picked a time for the afternoon. A day later, I arrived at a small office off Market Street. It was the office of Mrs. Thorstein, a fair-haired, bright-eyed woman of Danish descent. I took the bus, although Joseph had offered to drive me, but it was something I wanted to do for myself.

A bell rang when I entered the office. Inside, there was a waiting room with four small wooden chairs, a small center table with an assortment of magazines, and a bowl of cherry-flavored hard candies. There was a caladium plant in the corner, next to a door that opened abruptly.

"Hello there."

"Hi, uh, Mrs. Thorstein?"

"That's right. Do you have an appointment today?"

"I do, um, my name is Grace."

"Yes, hello Grace. It's a pleasure to meet you. Please come in."

She pulled the door wide open to her office, nearly knocking over the caladium in the process, and motioned for me to step in first. The office contained a dark brown old-fashioned lounge chair and a barrister bookshelf lined with self-help books and medical journals behind its smoked glass. She sat in front of me in a chair much like Henry's. The walls were painted a cool blue and the floor was hard wood with a prominent Persian rug laid upon it.

She sat behind a desk topped with a calendar, stress ball, timer, and a light-green candle that was lit next to it. Beside the candle was a steaming cup of tea.

"Would you like some tea?"

Set in my ways with coffee, I denied her offer.

"It's green tea, a blessing to the immune system. Antioxidants for the skin, eases digestion, calms the nerves."

I inhaled the aroma of the candle, which upon looking closer to it actually read *Green Tea*. It was a sweet but earthy smell, invigorating my senses. She had sold me.

"Actually, I'll have a cup, please."

She was pleased with my decision. She dipped below her desk and brought up a ridiculously large flask, a dainty white teacup, and a matching saucer. She grabbed a small green sachet and tossed it into the cup, delicately pouring the hot water over it. Placing the teacup on the saucer, she handed it over to me.

It was steaming, but not hot enough to set down and wait on. I grabbed the handle with two fingers, holding the saucer underneath, and took my first sip of it. It was pleasant, slightly bitter but not overpowering like a mug of black coffee was. A subtle, almost floral flavor lingered on my tongue afterward.

"So, Grace, how can I help you today?" she asked casually.

I looked around the room for a way to start. "Um, well, I—I think that . . . I think I might be . . ." A book to my left titled *Repairing Thought* came into my view. "I think that I might be . . . broken."

"I see." She took a sip of her tea and set the cup down onto her saucer. "And have you ever sought out any help like this before?"

I shook my head.

"Well, my name is Ida Thorstein, and I'm a licensed clinical psychologist. You can call me Ida, Mrs. Ida, Mrs. Thorstein, whichever you'd prefer."

On the wall behind her head, I noticed a framed Master's degree from Pennsylvania State University.

"You went to Penn State," I noted.

"Yes, I did. For six years," she announced.

"I just graduated from there."

"Oh really? What in?"

"English Literature."

"Ah, I bet you're an avid reader, hmm?"

I nodded.

"And you're a writer," she added.

I looked at her blue eyes and she quickly looked down to her desk.

"Yes, actually. How'd you guess?"

She turned toward her framed degree in her chair, surveying for a second, and then slowly moved back to face me.

"Grace, I want you to know that I pride myself in maintaining a high standard of confidentiality with my clients . . . but I want to be honest with you. I can't pretend that I don't know who you are."

I sighed. Honestly, it was a relief to hear.

"I saw you on the Studio 7 News just a while ago," she confessed.

"Oh, right," I muttered.

"I thought you were incredible, the way you opened up like that."

"Thank you."

"I'm really glad you're here, and I hope that you can be honest with me, too, and open up the way you did that morning."

I looked down at my tea and saw myself reflected in it. "I want to be," I replied, "but . . . I'm not sure if I'll be any good at it."

Ida tilted her head to the side while she observed my expression. "Well, let's try then. How old are you, Grace?"

"Twenty-two."

"Is that the truth?"

"Yes, of course."

"Great. So far so good."

I giggled quietly, and she smiled.

"Now, my turn. I'm forty-seven," she said, shrugging and raising her eyebrows.

I smiled back.

"Let's try another," she prodded.

I gazed around the room for a sentence. "I think I'm crazy," I said.

"Hmm. Well, I don't think you are." She added, "I think that you're hurting, and that it's been a problem for you for some time now."

I swallowed a lump in my throat.

"Your turn," she declared.

"I'm afraid," I revealed.

"I'd be concerned if you weren't."

"I just want to think straight again."

"Then I think you're in the right place."

I took another sip of tea and gave in to its calming effect. I opened my mind like a book and decided to give Ida my story like a publishing query. She listened intently, with no judgments or after thoughts, and scanned over my words like Henry did. Then, she gave it her approval and began her edits, like Nick did.

Sixty minutes of her time became sixty minutes of mining the lumps of coal in my head. I felt . . . relieved. It was the right thing for me, just as Emilia said. Ida analyzed me and brought up a lot of me that I didn't know existed.

I came to understand that the visions in my head, the night-mares, and the blackouts were all a result of post-traumatic stress disorder. It's a term I hadn't ever considered for myself. I'd never fought in any wars, after all. But, as Ida had told me, I had been long engaged in a war inside my head, all the way back to when I lost Sam.

I remember that after he slipped through my hands, I stumbled backward and vomited on the road. I thought it was just from the fumes of the burning underground, but it was an emotional reac-tion, and the start of my mental collapse. The nightmares began after that, as well as the daydreams, or "daymares," Ida called them. Even the night I met Joseph, I couldn't sleep because my mind was racing. I was stuck inside one of the nightmares.

She revealed the significance of the shaky hands, picking away at my scar until it bled, disassociating as I tapped a pen at my side until it left a mark, and the insatiable craving for coffee to keep me awake so I didn't have to relive it all in a nightmare. Most recently, too, the moment I had in the bathtub, where I let myself burn in the water. They were all coping mechanisms that I'd been entertaining subconsciously. It all made sense to me now, and I had an official diagnosis.

At first, I felt shame. But Ida urged me not to feel this way, to accept my trauma so that I could grow from it. She asked that I continue to see her, once a week. She also gave me some homework to do.

"I want you to keep a journal. Write when you're happy, sad, confused. Write when you feel yourself beginning to daydream, and when you wake up from a nightmare. And, Grace, if you can, try to limit yourself from drinking coffee."

Coffee to me was like quaaludes to my mother, not nearly as dangerous, but it was the same principle, and I felt sick with myself because of it. Ida left me with a journal and a small bag of assorted teas of the much less caffeinated variety: English breakfast tea to wake me up, the green tea to calm my nerves, and a herbal mixture of chamomile to help me sleep. It was a transition that I was willing to make, and I admit that the flavors were more to my taste anyway.

I decided to write the instant I got back home from the visit. I flashed through the French doors and scurried up the stairs to my typewriter.

"How was it?" Joseph asked, appearing from the kitchen.

I paused at the top of the stairs to look down to him. "It was better than I expected," I stated. "I'm going to do some writing now."

He flashed me that sweet smile and asked, "Hey, would you

want some coffee to go with it?"

"Actually, I'd *love* a cup of tea."

I threw down the bag of teas to Joseph, who caught them in a way that would make Sully proud, and found my way to the typewriter.

CHAPTER TWENTY-ONE

I MASTERED THE ART OF scribbling quietly at night, using only the moonlight to jot down my latest nightmare. One night, I had a dream that was particularly unnerving:

I'm lying in the middle of the road in my mother's black dress and I can't move. A cloud of smoke lingers all around me, and the road is melting into a bubbling black tar pit, semi-solid, and my body sticks to it. My skin is blistering against it, and I'm screaming for help.

"*Please!*" I cry out.

Suddenly, out of the smoke I see a dark silhouette appear, creeping toward me with precise, still movements. The shape moves closer to me in a haunting ballet of steps without making a sound. As it nears my body, I can make out what it is. It's a large buck, and it is alone.

With each step it takes, the earth around its hooves blossoms with lush moss, grasses, and small flowers, but as soon as each hoof rises from the ground, the grasses burn and crumble to ash. It blooms and burns, over and over, with the buck giving it life and taking it away with each step it takes closer to me. I can see pieces of ash surrounding the buck's head, floating through the air in the shape of little black butterflies that turn to dust as they near my body.

The buck is standing right in front of me on the road, looking me dead in the eyes, before lowering his head down, and offering his antlers to me. My hands are suddenly freed from the tar, and I grab onto the antlers. He's not afraid of me, and I'm not afraid of him. He begins to tread hard against the melting road, trying his best to pull me out. But my hands slip, and I fall down, deep down into the tar pit. That's when I woke up.

It was a massive load off my shoulders to write it all down, especially in the middle of the night, when I'd normally lie awake in bed and replay it over and over in my head like a broken record. I wrote it all down and there it stayed on the page. You'd think someone with a degree in English Literature would know to write about their obstacles, but I preferred running away from them my entire life. That feeling I had before, about being a butterfly undergoing metamorphosis, was stronger than ever now, and my journal was growing thicker as I filled it with my thoughts.

When my mind was emptied, I was able to go back to sleep, curling over toward Joseph and pulling his arm around me. I felt safe and peaceful hearing only the sounds of our breathing.

My days still started at seven o'clock as per usual. Since kicking my coffee habit for a healthier cup of black tea in the mornings, I had felt better. I had even found my favorite brand: a hot cup of Yorkshire Tea. It's an English breakfast tea accompanied by one teaspoon of sugar for that hint of sweetness I always delight in. And if I ever felt tired or anxious, I would instead go for a big glass of the nectar of life: water. When I got to work, I still poured a cup of coffee for Nick before heading straight to my desk. I still enjoyed the aroma.

One day, when I got to my desk today, I was shocked to find there were no queries. Not a single writer in the Philadelphia area had an idea they deemed fit for publishing that day.

"Well would you look at that. We're like a ghost town—I mean, like a desert," Nick said.

"Do you want another cup of joe?" I asked, fiddling around for something to do. "Or how about a nice cup of tea?"

I was becoming quite the advocate for tea drinking, but he gestured toward his mug and sipped away at it, full, dark, and aromatic.

I sat back down in my chair and began imagining myself on television again, only this time as a tea saleswoman in an advert.

Don't let coffee lead you astray, grab a nice cuppa, and make the switch today!

I began conducting a symphony in my head for the jingle that would go with it, beginning in tune of A-minor, when Nick interrupted my thoughts.

"You know what I would love?" Nick started.

My ridiculous train of thought had derailed.

"A nice new book to read."

I raised my eyebrows at the idea.

"Have you read my mystery novel yet?" he prodded.

"Actually, my father is reading it now."

"Oh, good!" he exclaimed.

"So, you haven't read anything interesting lately? I mean, not even here, at work?" I asked curiously.

"Well, sure. These manuscripts are worth the read, but the way I read through them is a little different than the way you would read a book on a rainy day. It's more technical work, really. I don't get involved in the stories." He ran a finger across the stack of scripts in front of him. "But, to tell the truth, it's been a while since I really had a good read, something that just keeps me up at night. Something gripping, enticing, pulling me in first thing at the end of a workday."

"Do you mean, a mystery novel?" I inquired.

"Anything, really. I don't judge a book by its cover. Sometimes a simple coffee-table read can have a greater impact than a bestselling suspenseful thriller."

I smiled at the thought of him intensely reading a small poetry book.

"But I'm happy that your father is enjoying my novel. I hope I can find my next good read soon, too."

He took a joyous swig of coffee and then scooted his chair forward, indicating that it was back to work for Nick. I turned toward my desk and thought about what he said: a new book would be a good idea. I didn't want to be left alone with my thoughts, so I pulled my journal out of my bag and flipped it open. As I was turning through my entries, I noticed I had written a substantial amount without even realizing it. It had all just bled out of me in the form of ink. I thought about what Ida said to me once: *It's better to have it freed onto paper, than trapped within the prison in your mind.*

It was advice that I had taken and been using for some time now. So, what if I started from the beginning? What if I emptied my mind onto paper, freeing all my thoughts in the form of a new book to read? What if . . . I wrote a memoir?

Ting!

Nick had returned the carriage on his typewriter back into place, and the little noise it made seemed to consummate the idea in my head. I looked above me in search of a floating light bulb.

When Nick was my English professor, he said that I had found an outlet in my writing, and it was true. He said it was something I'd always carry, but he and I had wanted me to outgrow it, to challenge myself into writing more, and expand my outlook on life.

But maybe, in order for me to grow, what if I *had* to write it all out? What if that was what I was meant to write about all along? First the article, and now Nick wanted a new book, and Stark Publishing could use a fresh idea. I glanced back over to Nick for some sort of affirmation, but he was miles away, absorbed in his work. So, I uncapped my pen and took a deep plunge into my mind, going all the way back to the start.

CHAPTER TWENTY-TWO

BY THE END OF THE DAY, my writing hand was cramping. I rubbed away at the soreness and wiggled my fingers. Nick threw in his daily end-of-work sigh and looked over to me.

"What have you been doing all this time?"

I shook my hand a little and closed my journal shut, bookmarking my place with my pen.

"Brainstorming," I proclaimed.

He raised his eyebrows and peered at my journal before I tucked it away in my bag. "Good to know," he said.

"It *sure* is," I said coyly, sweeping up my long hair into a ponytail. I could see Nick trying to make sense of my remark.

"You go ahead, Grace. I'll close up, and I'll see you Monday with your book of *ideas*."

He looked down to my bag and then back to me.

"That sounds like a plan. Thanks, Nick."

"Of course, and remember . . . as Mark Twain once said, the secret to getting ahead, is getting started."

"Huh, that's a new one. I'll remember that," I said.

I smiled at Nick, and he smiled back, then I walked out of the office. I headed out the door, quickly pulled out my journal, and jotted down that quote.

When I got home, I stood in the foyer alone. I slid off my shoes and hung my bag on the hook by the door, then I took my journal upstairs to my writing desk. Joseph wasn't in the bedroom, and he usually waits for me by the door. It was unusual.

"Joe?" I called.

I glanced over at my typewriter, tempted to tickle away at its keys, shook my head, and then headed downstairs. I overheard Joseph, Emilia, and Richard chatting away in the kitchen. When I walked in on them, they were pouring wine, red wine, pulled straight from the top of their wine shelf.

"Is that a vintage?" I asked, picking up on their sense of elation. "What's the occasion?"

"Grace," Joseph said. "You've *done* it!"

"I . . . did? Did what?"

"Grace, the mayor called. They tallied the votes. Centralia is *finished!*"

Time was pulling me by the hand into another dimension again. Only this time it was to a higher one, one where gods and goddesses governed the realm. I was ascending. Richard poured me a glass of the wine, and Emilia pulled me in for a hug and a kiss on the cheek.

"Oh, honey, we are *so, so* happy for you."

I saw a flash in my mind of that man in the meeting with his gray face and blue overalls. He was on his knees, begging me for forgiveness.

"It's about *damn* time," Richard declared, holding a glass in the air.

I just stood there with my mouth hanging open, shaking my head. Maybe it was a daydream. Maybe I was imagining things, and maybe I should write this all down.

"Evacuation protocols are already in place," Joseph said while placing both hands on my shoulders. "This is *real*, Grace. It's really happening."

He stole a kiss from me, and I melted into a puddle in his hands.

I looked down to my glass and saw my reflection again. A happy woman looked back at me, blushing pink and smiling wide. She looked like she was on top of the world. The first thing I could think to say was, "I have to tell Bill. Please, excuse me for just a moment."

"Go on, dear. We'll be waiting in the living room," Emilia said, and the three of them left me with some privacy.

When I was sure I was alone, I pressed my head against the wall, giggling and smiling like a child. Centralia was soon to be nevermore, a blank space on the earth, condemned to damnation. Hell's gates were closing for good, and Hades, great god of the underworld, was finally retiring beneath.

I dialed the number for Bill, quickly and impatiently, and it rang three times before he picked up.

"Hello?"

"Dad!"

"Hey, kiddo! How are you?"

"Dad, are you sitting down?"

I heard him slump into a seat.

"Well, I am now. What's going on, Grace?"

"There's something I have to tell you."

"Sure, shoot."

"Dad, Centralia is being evacuated. I mean, *permanently*. Pennsylvania is going to fill in the town with dirt!"

After a moment of silence, Bill uttered a jumbled ball of sounds before he could form his first sentence.

"Grace, how did—how is this happening?"

"There was a town meeting I attended a few weeks ago. I—I didn't tell you because I didn't want you to think about it. But Dad, the county passed the decision today!"

"A town meeting? Oh, good Lord, Grace. Grace! Did you do this, kiddo?"

I pulled the phone away for a moment, looking up to the

heavens, before saying, "It was all meant to be, Dad."

"I can't believe it. This is real?"

"Yes, it's real!"

There was a pause on Bill's end.

"Dad?"

"I'm here, Grace."

"What, what's wrong? Aren't you happy?"

"I am, Grace. I am, really. It's just, your mother . . . she . . ." His voice became breathy and distant. "She never would have left it, you know, even after hearing this."

I sighed into the phone, and I could hear him coiling the phone line on his end. "I know, Dad. I know."

He sighed back into the phone with me, and we stood there in silence for a minute, still connected, before he spoke again.

"Grace?"

"Yeah, Dad?

"I'm happy."

I closed my eyes and felt my heart beating slowly in my chest. "I'm happy you're happy." I could almost hear a smile on his face through the phone line when he asked, "So, what now, kiddo?"

A smile spread over my face as well. "You have to come and celebrate with us! Please, what are you doing now?"

"I'll be there in twenty minutes." He hung up on me, but it didn't even matter because I was the epitome of joy. I glided into the living room and joined Joseph on the couch.

"When is he coming?" Joseph asked, reading my mind again.

"Twenty minutes!"

Time flew, and before long Bill arrived.

"Hello?" he called out.

I sprung up from the couch like a rabbit and rushed over to him, jumping into his arms. He twirled me around and around like I was a kid again. I dropped to my feet, and we embraced tightly, laughing

laughing and grinning and welling up.

My family, my loving family, who'd supported me since the start, all gathered around Bill and me, joining in our jubilation. I felt like Dorothy from *The Wizard of Oz* again, reunited with her folks having clicked my heels together.

There's no place like home, there's no place like home.

No, there wasn't a home like it anymore. Centralia was nothing but a memory to us now, an epitaph on a tombstone, a flame that can be blown out.

I write every day now, and I've submitted another publishing query to Henry for my memoir. With ready hands, Nick awaits my finished work to begin his edits, and Henry waits for another book to add to his shelf of trophies beside the admirable Mark Twain.

As of today, Centralia has been fully evacuated. Every home is empty, and the corner shop has closed for good. The mining tunnels will be the first to be filled in, to completely seal it off from the world above. The houses and abandoned buildings will be torn down carefully, with only limited contractors, laborers, and equipment allowed on the weak ground at one time. The last step will be a layer of dirt to bury the town completely. Once that is finished, the main road will be closed off for good.

Bill has joined a project called "One Liberty Place" and is due to start construction on it soon. He boasts that it will be the tallest skyscraper in Philadelphia; a complete turnaround from the deep pits of the mining tunnels. It's the kind of building Sam would have designed, he says.

Joseph has received a promotion working under his father and is earning enough money for us to move into our own apartment, too, splitting rent equal ways with me and continuing to swap cooking dinner on rotating nights.

I continue to see Ida, and I'm getting close to needing a second journal. I've also taken up an entire kitchen cabinet with a variety of different teas that she's recommended.

When I look in the mirror, I see that happy woman staring back at me, no longer clinging to the past or trying to bury it away in her mind. I have grown a lifetime in the last few years. I still see the buck in my sleep sometimes, and he is a welcome presence now, free to roam the space in my dreams. I've fought for my family and for the future generations of Pennsylvania, and I will continue to fight my demons. I've accepted the life that I have lived, and I have risen from the ashes like a phoenix.

EPILOGUE – ELLIE

I HEARD MY DADDY SLAM THE DOOR SHUT. He was talking to another man on the porch, for the third day in a row now. I don't know what they were talking about, but I know it made my daddy start shoutin'. I'm not allowed to go out there.

Him and my mama were arguing in the kitchen about some girl they saw on the TV.

"If it weren't for that stupid little girl . . . and who does she think she is, living in the big city on her high horse?"

I don't know who she is or what kind of horse she has, but my mama and daddy really don't like her, or the man on the porch.

"They're giving us a *grace period* before we have to leave. Did they really have to go and put it like that?" he shouted.

My mama turned toward me.

"Now, Ellie, we're gonna have to go away for a little while. Like a vacation, to the outside."

"But, I don't wanna go outside, Mama."

"Yes, sweetie, I know, but this is what we have to do now."

"But, why?"

"Because we have to, Ellie. Come on, let's get you to bed."

"Mama, where's my stick?"

"Honey, be a dear and grab Ellie's cane?"

"Here you go, sweetie."

My stick helps me walk. I can't see so well anymore, but I can still hear them fighting from my room.

"Jesus, what are we going to do, David? Where are we supposed to go?"

"Hell if I know. That little *bitch* has no idea what she's done."

"What about Ellie? She hasn't ever set a foot outside. How are we going to live?"

"Dammit, Cathy, I said I don't know. What the hell do I know about being blind? Want me to close my eyes and figure it all out for you?"

"We *can't* leave, David!"

"Well, we *have* to!"

I don't know why, or where we're going, but my mama keeps saying that the outside is hard for people like me. She says that they have to go to school. She says it's a lot of money for people like me, and my daddy keeps yelling at her about it.

I wish they would stop fighting. I don't wanna go nowhere. I don't want my daddy to run outta money either.

"Are we fools? To think we could've raised her like this?"

"Now you just stop. You know damn well that we can't afford special schooling for her. We've done everything we can to keep her safe here."

"What will we tell her? She's eight years old, David. Think about how this will hurt her."

"How *she* hurt her, that damned Grace, and to think I shared my town with her . . . out here preaching about saving the children, when she doesn't even know the *half* of it."

"Well, what if we don't leave? What if we just stay, David? We're doin' fine here. They can't *really* force us out, can they?"

"They can, Cathy. And they will."

"We're goin' to be on the streets, aren't we?"

"I don't know, honey. I don't know."

I hate hearing my mama cry. She'd never sounded like this

before in my whole life. I guess her name is Grace, the girl from the TV. I think she's making us leave for the outside.

But I don't wanna go outside.

ABOUT THE AUTHOR

SYDNEY WALTERS is an author, press release writer, and digital marketer from Washington, DC. She writes for numerous publications, including *Your Health Magazine* and *The Prompt*, and also maintains a beauty blog for a local hair salon. Short stories, sappy love poems, and clever birthday cards are some of her lesser-known works.

Fascinated by ghost towns from an early age, Sydney is now an avid explorer of ruins and abandoned places around the globe, including Centralia, Pennsylvania. The town's history and cultural impact—serving as the inspiration for the horror franchise *Silent Hill*—moved Sydney to write her own take on it, and thus, *State of Grace* was born.

Acts of Grace is the second in a series centered around historical events told from a young woman's perspective.